ONCE IN AWHILE

ONCE IN AWHILE

KAY G. JAY

TATE PUBLISHING
AND ENTERPRISES, LLC

This novel is a work of fiction. Names, descriptions, entities, and incidents included in the story are products of the author's imagination. Any resemblance to actual persons, events, and entities is entirely coincidental.

The opinions expressed by the author are not necessarily those of Tate Publishing, LLC.

Published by Tate Publishing & Enterprises, LLC
127 E. Trade Center Terrace | Mustang, Oklahoma 73064 USA
1.888.361.9473 | www.tatepublishing.com

Tate Publishing is committed to excellence in the publishing industry. The company reflects the philosophy established by the founders, based on Psalm 68:11,
"The Lord gave the word and great was the company of those who published it."

Cover design by Joshua Rafols
Interior design by Richell Balansag

Published in the United States of America

ISBN: 978-1-68301-514-7
1. Fiction / Action & Adventure
2. Fiction / Thrillers / Espionage
16.04.26

This goes out to my family and friends
for they are truly my *merry band of misfits*

1

THE DARK FIGURE was shrouded in a brown hooded robe; the face hidden in darkness. It began moving menacingly toward her. She whirled around frantically, looking for a way to escape. Finding none, she stumbled backwards, hitting the wall behind her. She slid down and cowered like a child as she waited for the inevitable attack by this faceless enemy. The room became deathly quiet. She slowly pulled her hands from her face and looked up. The face, only inches from hers, seized her heart in sheer terror and tore a primal scream from the center of her soul.

He leapt from the couch where he had fallen asleep and ran for the door. The gunshot wound he sustained a few weeks earlier pulled as he stumbled headlong into the main foyer and scrambled up the large central staircase, turning left at the landing. The colonial-style house was divided into two apartments. He reached the other apartment's second floor balcony at a dead run and threw his weight against the wooden door. It gave easily under his force, and he rolled into the room. Leaping to his feet, chest heaving, he was prepared to do battle. He swiftly surveyed the room. Finding no obvious enemy, he went to the woman on the floor who was curled in a fetal position, crying softly. She had not stirred. Bending over, he touched her gently on the shoulder. She sprang to life. He easily deflected her fist strike aimed at his jaw but he did not anticipate the foot that drove into his groin. He squeaked her name as he toppled over. Despite the slightly higher octave, she knew that voice. She hurriedly knelt beside the man. His normally tanned skin looked a little pasty in the moonlight. He stared straight up at the ceiling.

He never blinked but finally croaked, "Kenann, you're killing me."

"Danny Mac, I didn't mean to kick you in the nuts."

He turned his eyes to her in mild disdain. "Well, thank you for putting it so delicately, but that is not what I meant." He slowly rolled on his side and made his way to a sitting position on the side of the bed. He patted the quilt for her to sit beside him. She complied. "Kenann, if you would just stop this nonsense and marry me, we could sleep together and I wouldn't have to break my neck trying to protect you."

"Well, for one thing, I don't need you to protect me. And for another, I don't think it's nonsense to have a proper dating period before we jump into marriage." Her normally curly hair was exceptionally wild, and her eyes blazed at him. He couldn't help it. She made him laugh. His eyes sparkled as he turned to her with a devastating smile. "And just what are you smiling about?" she huffed.

"You."

"What's so funny?"

"I repeat."

"First you want to marry me, then you make fun of me."

"I'm not making fun of you, sweetheart, but I am having all kinds of fun *with* you."

"Hardy har har!" She slapped his bare shoulder. "Hey, what are you doing here anyway?"

"Well, when I hear a bloodcurdling scream, I'm inclined to investigate."

"I screamed?"

"Yes, and you were so out of it you never flinched when I busted in here. It wasn't till I touched you that you came out swinging."

"Are you all right? I really didn't mean to hurt you."

"Yeah, sure. First, you reject my proposal of marriage, then you try to crush my manhood."

"I did not reject your proposal, Danny Mac."

"I'm just messing with you."

"Well, quit it."

"You were also crying. What were you dreaming about?"

The dream flooded back. She clamped down on renewed terror. "I have no idea," she lied.

"Well, it isn't like you haven't had some traumatic experiences lately. It's probably just leftover nerves. Get back to sleep." Danny Mac stood to return to his apartment. "Coming over for breakfast?"

"Yeah, I guess." Her voice held a pout.

He turned. "What's the matter?"

"You haven't kissed me nearly enough since we left Egypt." She thought that might take her mind off the dream that had burned itself into her brain.

"Kenann, passion has never been our problem. At some point, you will have to trust that I love you for who you are and I'll love you forever."

"Well, can't you just give me one little kiss?"

"No, because it won't end there, especially alone in this bedroom in the middle of the night. I am only human. Go to sleep."

She really needed a distraction. She walked over and put her arms around his neck, smiling up at him. She played with the back of his hair. He looked to the ceiling as if appealing for strength then looked down at her and smiled. He slowly bent his head to hers. Her face turned up to meet his lips, she curled her fingers in his hair. As he deepened the kiss, she felt his arms tightening and pressing her to him. Oh yeah, she was definitely distracted. He turned with her and pressed her against the door. Pulling her arms over her head, he plundered her mouth. He felt the point of no return rolling over him and forced himself to slow down. While her mind surged with powerful feelings, he lightened the kiss and slowly lifted his mouth from hers. He pulled their hands down and squeezed her shoulders. He kissed her forehead and stepped back.

"Now go to sleep."

"Of all people, why did I have to fall for a preacher?"

He laughed and moved away from her. He winked at her before closing the door. Returning to his apartment, his mind replayed the events that had brought him and Kenann to this point in their lives.

Daniel MacKenzie, an orphan from Oklahoma with obvious Native American ancestry, had trained as a Marine and had become proficient in strategy and death. He came in contact—in some cases, intimately—with some unsavory characters during those years. He eventually became sickened by all he had seen and done and turned to Jake, his former commander who had become an elder in the church here in Memphis. Danny Mac gave himself and his life to God and eventually became the minister for the Memphis congregation that met across the street from this duplex apartment.

His former life though, would not lie dormant. A former lover sent her minions to kidnap him. She wanted him to help her overtake a secret society that had powerful contacts in every country in the world. In order to control Danny Mac, they had orders to also kidnap someone close to him as insurance. Kenann James had recently moved into the duplex beside Danny Mac. They had become friends; but to those who observed them, it appeared they were lovers and living together in the Colonial-style house. When they moved in to take Danny Mac, they took Kenann to ensure his cooperation.[1*]

During the ordeal, passion flared between them while Danny Mac struggled with his vows of purity. Kenann knew in her heart that when Danny Mac said he loved her, he meant it; but she could not shake the fear that they had been caught up in the situation and his feelings might not last. Now that they were safely home, she pushed for a dating period. Danny Mac insisted they already knew what they wanted but gave into her wishes and tried to be patient.

He smiled as he remembered their friends who had gone to Alexandria, Egypt, and the desert beyond, to rescue them. Andrew O'Hanlon was his buddy from the Marines who now worked for the CIA. He headed up the government's contingency to rescue them; but he received considerable, often unwelcome, help from some zealous civilians. Their former commander now church elder, Jake Taylor, tagged along to keep his eye on Mrs. Gabrielle Gage. She was an enigmatic and wealthy widow with a penchant for romance and intrigue; most of which, she has lived out in her own mysterious life. She constantly amazed them all with her contacts and resources. Judy Crawford, Kenann's best friend, had fought her own demons in order to plunge into the

---

[1*] See Book 1: *Once A Long Time Ago*

rescue effort and proved invaluable with her skills as a nurse, her tough nature, and her punch-you-in-the-gut beauty, which did not go unnoticed by Andy O'Hanlon.

Blade, a ten-year-old boy, stowed away on their rescue plane because he wanted to help Danny Mac. Mrs. Gage almost turned the plane around until Jake pointed out that Blade's dark skin from an African American father and a Filipino mother would be of help on the African continent. Last but not the least in the contingency, was Danny Mac's newest best friend, Moira James, Kenann's grandmother. She was a tiny woman with long peach-colored hair—the combination of ginger and silver—usually worn in a long braid. She was born in Waterford, Ireland, and came to America with her Welsh husband. She had lost him, her only son, and her daughter-in-law to early deaths. Kenann was all she had in the world, except for an unwavering faith in God and a touch of the Irish second sight. When she sensed something wrong with her granddaughter, she took a fast flight from West Virginia and would not be dissuaded from tagging along on the rescue mission.

Danny Mac and Granny James had not met until the ordeal was concluded; but it was love at first sight. He now looked forward to his daily calls to West Virginia. Sometimes it is just to chat; other days, he is begging for advice on how to handle her headstrong granddaughter.

2

KENANN ROLLED OUT of bed the next morning feeling groggy and disheveled. One look in the mirror confirmed both. She exited the shower a few minutes later, towel-drying her hair. She flipped her head over and finger combed the curly mass. That and a little gel were the extent of her efforts at style and headed downstairs to meet Danny Mac for breakfast.

He really was being patient with her. She must be nuts not to jump at his offer of marriage. He was everything a woman could want. But that was just it; for the life of her, she could not figure out why he chose her. He had naturally dark skin with aquiline features and the light eyes of European ancestry. She liked to tease him about his good looks because it made him very uncomfortable. She suspected he thought them a nuisance. He also worked very hard to hide the tough side to his nature. He wanted to keep that dark and dangerous part of his life buried in his past. Despite his best efforts, it remained just below the surface.

As Kenann hit the floor of the central foyer between the two apartments, the front door burst open. A boy, gliding on the rug, slid in sideways and came to a perfect stop in front of Kenann. They both extended their right hands and began an elaborate maneuver of bumps, slaps, and sliding of palms and fingers. It was their own signature handshake.

"Hey, Blade. You here for breakfast too?"

"French toast?"

"I hope so. Let's go find out."

She slung her arm around the boy's shoulders and once again thanked the good Lord for bringing him home safely from that sacrificial slab in the desert of Egypt. They opened the double doors into Danny Mac's living room. Since the house had originally been a single dwelling, the entrance to both apartments consisted of matching oak-paneled double doors. One side had been the parlor and the other had been the formal dining room. Now they were converted into living spaces with attached dining areas in each side. Danny Mac's side held the original and the largest kitchen while Kenann's apartment was equipped with a smaller galley kitchen and breakfast nook overlooking their large tree-shaded backyard. The area beneath and behind the main central stairs was divided into the first floor bathrooms for both apartments.

Danny Mac heard them come in and came through the swinging door from the kitchen wearing an apron and oven mitts. "Good morning, ladies and gentleman. If you'll have a seat, your gustatory experience will begin."

Kenann laughed and pulled Blade toward the dining table sitting in the sunlight of the front window. There were three place settings laid.

Blade whispered, "What is *gussidory*?"

"I think that means eatin' good in the neighborhood'."

Danny Mac carried out a tray laden with French toast, strawberries, powdered sugar, and syrup. On the table was a carafe for coffee and a glass pitcher with orange juice.

Blade rubbed his hands together. "Let's dig in and *gussidory*."

"Not so fast, buddy. Let's say our thanks first."

Everything happened at once. They all heard what sounded like a gunshot. With lightning speed, Danny Mac grabbed them by their collars, pulled them to the floor, and covered their bodies with his own. Kenann felt his heart pounding on her back. He slowly moved off them while motioning them to stay down. He went to the window. Nothing seemed out of the ordinary. People were casually going about their business on the sidewalk outside. He turned back and looked at Kenann, who was sitting up by now.

"Danny Mac, I think it was a car backfiring."

"Yeah, I guess so." He continued to look troubled.

"Wow, that was exciting. Can we eat now?"

Danny Mac gave a shaky smile to his little friend.

"Sure, buddy." He reached out and pulled Kenann and Blade to their feet. He righted the chairs, and they all sat down again.

"Father, thank you for this day you have given us. Thank you for this food. Keep us from harm. Protect us from the evil one. Lead us in your way. In Jesus's name, amen."

Blade gave an enthusiastic *amen* and reached for the French toast. Kenann looked across at Danny Mac and gave an inquisitive lift to her eyebrow. Danny Mac shrugged a shoulder. He was obviously still very edgy from their ordeal over the summer.

Katarina, his former lover and compatriot, was dead. Pierre, the leader of the society she was trying to overtake, had been killed as well. Pierre Montfort was convinced upon seeing Kenann for the first time that she was the reincarnated Sumerian goddess, Inanna, come to fulfill the long-awaited prophecy of their ancient society. The climax of the ordeal had occurred in a subterranean cavern in the Sahara Desert. A sacrifice of blood was required, which is how Blade ended up on that stone altar. Danny Mac killed Pierre, Kenann killed Katerina, and Danny Mac took a bullet meant for Angelo.

Angelo had been one of the best things to come out of the entire ordeal. Danny Mac had been Angelo's enemy for almost ten years. But as Angelo kept close video surveillance on Danny Mac and Kenann while they were held captive, he became enthralled by the change in Danny Mac and the things he discussed with Kenann. He began to question his own life's values, and when Danny Mac leapt to shield him from a bullet meant for him, Angelo was changed. He returned to Alexandria with a band of friends and was at Danny Mac's bedside every day. He learned about the Son of God while Danny Mac convalesced and provided Andy with all the information he had at his disposal about the society. He had resigned himself to imprisonment for his partnership with Katarina, despite his efforts to thwart her near the end. When Andy and Danny Mac gave him his chance for freedom, he was stunned and humbled.

He asked, "Why are you doing this?"

Andy shrugged and grinned, pointing to Danny Mac. "He's gone soft in his old age."

Danny Mac reached out to grasp Angelo's hand. Angelo slowly put his hand in Danny Mac's and squeezed. Danny Mac returned the gesture.

"One who was once my enemy is now my friend."

Angelo replied, "I will never forget this, Danny. Never."

"Just keep searching for truth, my friend. That's all I ask."

"I will. I will." He took the train ticket from Andy with a new passport bearing the name of David Saul along with the Bible inscribed by Danny Mac. He walked away from them slowly. He looked back over his shoulder and smiled the smile of his youth. Danny Mac thought it was the most beautiful thing he had ever seen next to Kenann when she laughs.

"We're taking a big chance, my friend." Andy had held some reservations about helping Angelo get away. His job would probably be on the line; but he had learned a long time ago to trust Danny Mac's instincts. He wasn't planning to quit now.

"Life is all about chances, Andy. We just gave that man a second one."

Danny Mac had heard from Angelo, aka David, that week. He was going to have to get used to calling him by his new name. He was doing well in Brussels. He had gotten a job at a firm that manufactured electronic equipment and had a small flat along the Seine. He had also reached out to some Christians about whom Danny Mac had told him. David thanked him again for his trust in him and for saving his life. Danny Mac chided him that their conversations were going to get pretty boring if they didn't find something else to talk about. David laughed and told him to always know that gratitude would be in his heart even if he did not speak of it. Danny Mac assured him he would hold him in his heart as well.

All was right with the world so why was he still so edgy. Something was off; but for the life of him, he couldn't put his finger on it. Maybe he would call Andy and see if something was up with their efforts to round up the society. It was a pretty monumental task being undertaken by the CIA, Interpol, and Mossad. Considering that this society claimed to have been in existence since the dawn of civilization and instrumental in the rise and fall of all major powers from Babylon to Rome to Hitler, it should be making front page news. But not one ripple had been leaked. That told him how serious this situation had been.

As they were clearing away the breakfast dishes, the phone rang. Danny Mac set down the stack of plates he was carrying and answered it.

The whining voice on the other end came on the line. "Daniel, it has come to my attention that the young lady living with you in that house is now your betrothed."

"Good morning, Mrs. Pettigrew. How are you feeling?"

"Don't try to change the subject, young man. Are you or are you not living in sin?"

"No, Ma'am, I am not."

"Who is to say what goes on behind those closed doors?"

"I do."

Mrs. Pettigrew paused, not knowing how to counter that simple statement without outright calling him a liar. She was not prepared to do that; but she was also not prepared to let it go either.

"Well, young man, mark my word. This will lead to no good."

"I appreciate your concern, Mrs. Pettigrew. I pray that everything behind your door is in good order. You have a really good day."

She harrumphed and hung up.

Kenann followed him into the kitchen with the last of the dishes. "What was that about?"

"Mrs. Pettigrew doing what she does best."

"Which is?"

"Meddling."

"Was it about us?"

Danny Mac looked at her and thought about being evasive but her eyes always compelled him.

"Yes."

"I wondered how long it would be before people began talking about us living here together."

"We are not living together, Kenann."

"You know what I mean. People are bound to wonder."

"People need to learn to trust each other a little bit and give the benefit of the doubt before they become judge and jury."

"Maybe I should move out."

"No!" Danny Mac nearly shouted.

Kenann came to him and touched her hand to his cheek. "Danny Mac, what's the matter?"

"I don't want you away from me. I want to be able to get to you in a hurry if you need me."

She framed his face with her hands. "Danny Mac, I am fine. We are fine. Please don't worry."

Danny Mac pulled Kenann into his arms and thanked God for this woman who had stolen his heart. He tipped her head up and bent slowly toward her lips. Her eyes widened in surprise.

He whispered, "Last night made me hungry for more."

"If Mrs. Pettigrew heard that she would—"

He captured her mouth, making the kiss count. Kenann's fingers curled in Danny Mac's shirt to hold herself upright. He raised his head at last.

"Wow!" Kenann sighed.

Danny Mac grinned. "Who do you want to listen to? Mrs. Pettigrew or me?

"Depends. Is she a good kisser?

Danny Mac shoved her head back with the palm of his hand. "Oh man, now that's in my head. Thanks."

Kenann cracked up. She began sparring with him and punched him in the stomach. "Oh, come on, tough guy. Can't take it?"

Danny Mac got a predatory look in his eye. Kenann knew that look and ran away screaming. Blade was watching TV in the living room but jumped up to join in the fun when she ran through the room with Danny Mac in hot pursuit. They ended up running around the yard and falling in a heap of laughter. Kenann was satisfied to see the lines of worry had left his face.

3

KENANN HAD YET to go back to work. She had just gotten a job as a therapist at a local counseling center when she was abducted with Danny Mac. Her boss had been apprised of the situation and had covered for her while she was gone. She met with him upon her return, and he asked her to take some more time before she came back to work. She was not sure that was a good idea; but he was insistent and placed her on paid medical leave. He told her he owned the company and he would do what he liked.

She felt fine most days; then out of the blue, she would weird out on herself. If she told anyone that she was seeing things, she would definitely not be going back to work unless it was to have one of them commit her to the psych unit. Her training had taught her the effects of extreme stress on the mind but she could not reconcile that with what she was experiencing. Danny Mac was having his own delayed stress reaction; but *she* was hallucinating. She had no intention of telling anyone *that*.

She mentally puts her fingers in her ears and sang, "La, la, la, la." No, she would handle this. One way or the other.

She was awakened by her name. No, not *her* name. Inanna. Had she dreamed it? She lay there for a moment as she allowed her racing heart to settle a bit. She sat up, still listening in the dark for more direction. *Direction? Where did that come from?* The voice had come from inside her room. She planted her feet on the floor and reached for her robe. She slipped it on and went down the spiral stairs that connected her galley kitchen and breakfast nook below. She was drawn outside into the moonlit night.

A privacy fence framed the sides of their backyard with a wooded area, creating the back boundary. The moon had turned the shadows blue, and she wanted to go there. The woods looked so inviting. She needed to be in those woods. She was vaguely aware of the damp grass beneath her feet. She saw the shadow man at the edge of the tree line and knew that was where she needed to go.

Suddenly, a large yellow dog blocked her path. She stopped and made eye contact with the dog, which then stood directly in front of her, planted its feet firmly, and bared its teeth at the shadow man. The shadow man started to move toward her. The dog went wild—leaping, growling, and barking; all the while, keeping itself between Kenann and this shadow man. The shadow man saw a light turn on at the back door and slipped back into the night.

Kenann fell to the ground. The dog ran after the shadow man. The good man would keep Kenann safe now.

Danny Mac's heart stopped when he saw Kenann's crumpled form lying in the wet grass at the tree line. He ran to her and kept calling her name as he pulled her into his arms. He was relieved to see her breath turning to vapor as she exhaled; but she did not open her eyes. He lifted her limp form and ran back to the house. He brought her to his couch and wrapped her in the blanket draped on the back of the couch.

As he rubbed her hands and arms, her eyelids fluttered open. "Danny Mac?"

"How do you feel? Do you hurt anywhere?"

"No. What are you doing?"

"I found you lying in the backyard."

She looked toward the front window and saw it was dark. "What time is it?"

"It's 3:00 a.m. What were you doing out there?"

"I don't know." She sat up, pulling the blanket close to her. "I must have been sleepwalking."

"If that dog barking and growling hadn't woken me up, it is hard to say how long you would have been lying out there. You are staying here tonight."

"Danny—" she tried to protest.

"No. That is final. Now take off that robe. It is wet." She obeyed. "Is your gown wet too?"

"No, Danny, it's fine."

"Here, lie down. Is this blanket warm enough?"

"Yes, Danny Mac. Quit fussing over me."

"Shut up." But he softened it with a smile. He pulled the ottoman in front of his arm chair and stretched out.

Her eyes were closed but she said after a few minutes, "I can't sleep with you staring at me."

"Too bad. You're lucky I don't put a bell around your neck."

She opened her eyes slightly and glared at him under hooded lids.

"Good night, Kenann."

"Good night, Danny Mac." She smiled and turned over to block out the sound of his concern.

Judy dropped her suitcase in the middle of the floor and went to her answering machine. Her time at home with her parents had been healing. She sorted through the various messages, disappointed that the one she wanted was not there. She couldn't blame him. She certainly had not given him any reason to pursue her since the end of the summer ordeal. Besides, Andy was a very busy man working for the CIA. He also had a way with women so he had probably moved on from whatever flirtatious feelings he had felt for her this summer.

She sighed and walked toward her kitchen to get something to drink. It was then she spied the envelope on the floor. She had overlooked it when she came in; but someone had obviously slipped it through an old dog flap in her back door. She bent to pick it up, not recognizing the handwriting. She could not stop her heart from beating faster as she opened it and pulled out a single sheet of paper. She sat down at the table as she read.

Dear Judy,

I am no good at this so please do not hold my fumbling attempts against me. I know you needed time; and I wanted to give it to you. I found out from Kenann that you were going home to your parents, and I couldn't stand not contacting you any longer. I am staying in town until I hear from you. How pathetic is this sounding to you? Because this is sounding very pathetic to me. I can't help it. I need you to tell me if we have a chance or if I need to take my pathetic self off somewhere to brood like

Heathcliff. I am at the Carlisle. It is not the moors, but I am calling your name across the mighty Mississippi.

Andrew

She laughed and clutched the paper to her chest. A plan began forming in her mind.

4

KENANN WALKED BACKWARDS, leading Danny Mac by the hand and admonishing him to keep his eyes closed. She glanced over her shoulder to get her bearings and he smacked his face into a tree. He brought his hand up to massage his cheek but was faithful to not open his eyes.

"Sorry about that!" Kenann giggled. "Here, let me turn around and you put your hands on my shoulders." A few minutes later, she stopped him. She guided him to sit down on a fallen tree. She got him situated and sat beside him. "Okay, you can open your eyes now."

Danny Mac slowly brought his eyes into focus. He was still for a few minutes, and Kenann began to fear she had miscalculated. Finally, he turned to her and said, "It's perfect."

She smiled in return. "It is, isn't it?"

They both surveyed their surroundings and could feel themselves begin to relax. They had traversed a narrow trail down from the dirt road after she parked her car in the grass. Beneath the canopy of the trees, the sun shone on the ground, in dappling shades of green and shimmering yellow. Across the path was a flat grassy area with a sloping bank leading to a small stream, perfect for a blanket and picnic basket. Their view from the log was of a rocky waterfall spilling over into a deep pool surrounded by ferns and vegetation. The stream continued its journey into the Mississippi River, glistening off in the distance through the trees. It was a secluded spot that made one feel secure from that outside world, with all its danger and sadness.

"How on earth did you find this place?"

"Oh, I just came upon it in my wanderings last week."

"And just why are you wandering?"

"Have you ever felt like you were coming out of your skin? Or the walls were closing in?"

He merely nodded, waiting on her to continue.

"Well, I was having one of those days…and voila! I found this place."

"Kenann, we haven't talked much about what happened. Maybe we need to."

"What is there to say?"

"I know you are a good counselor, but you are a lousy one to yourself. Of course, some things need to be talked about. For goodness' sake, you killed someone."

"So did you."

"Unfortunately for me, it was not the first time. I don't necessarily want to think about it anymore than you do, but we need to. It is haunting your dreams. Every time I think about how close you and Blade came to getting hurt or killed, my heart stops. And I dream too."

"You never said anything."

"Well, I am saying it now."

Kenann sighed deeply. "I feel like I'm losing my mind. Nothing seems normal to me. That's why I think we should wait before we make anything final between us."

"Are you having doubts?"

"No, but I am not sure about anything else. And I am afraid that is not a good foundation to start on."

He refused to respond to this line of thinking and chose to ignore it. "Why do you feel like you are losing your mind?"

"Don't you? I jump at the slightest noise. I see shadows where there are none."

"Kenann, are you sure you have no memory of what took you into the backyard last night?"

She saw the look of fear and concern in his eyes and couldn't tell him the truth. She knew it was more than simple sleepwalking. Something was happening to her; and she didn't know what it was. How could she tell him she found herself responding to voices in her head? Things she knew were not from her. She would be fine but then, out of the blue it seemed, she was gone. She would come back to herself later, feeling drained and exhausted. She saw the hideous face from her dreams and shuddered.

"Cold?"

"No." She finished laying out their picnic blanket. He stretched out across from her and grabbed a pepperoni roll.

"I love these things. Did you make them?"

"Yep, believe it or not. It's a staple from West Virginia."

"See, you *can* cook."

"In a pinch." She laughed, opened up a can of Coke, and passed it to him.

"Kenann, what is going on with you?"

"What do you mean?"

"Don't play dumb. You are troubled and keeping something from me. What is it?"

"You said it yourself we have been through a lot. That's all it is." Her thoughts warred within her. If she was going to marry him, she knew she had to trust him. But about this—not yet.

Danny Mac watched her face and the emotions dancing across it. He would let it go for now. "Let's finish our lunch and enjoy the peace and quiet for a bit. I have to go to the hospital this afternoon and then do some studying for class tonight."

"I wish I could go back to work but Mr. Kesselring is adamant. Do you think he knows something I don't?"

"I don't know about that but I do think you need to talk to someone. If it's not me, that's okay." He added quickly before she could protest, "You do need to talk to someone."

Kenann considered this for a few minutes and conceded. "I suppose you're right. But who?"

"That is more your department, honey."

Granny. It came to Kenann at that moment. Why had she not thought of her before? Granny knows her better than any person alive. She will know what to do. This brought a sense of relief, and she smiled at Danny Mac.

He smiled back. "We will get through this, babe," he said.

"Yes, we will."

5

ANDY PACED BACK and forth in his hotel room. He purposely did not let Danny Mac know he was in town. If Judy was going to reject him, he wanted to lick his wounds in private. This waiting was intolerable. Had she received his letter? What would she do? Maybe he should just go back to DC today and forget it. The feelings he thought he had felt from her were probably only wishful thinking anyway.

He flopped into the chair and sat sulking by the window when a knock came at the door. He leapt to his feet and was at the door in seconds. He stopped and made himself take a deep breath. He was embarrassed to see his hand tremble as he reached for the handle.

His smile turned to puzzlement when he was met by a delivery man who held out a clipboard to him. "Sign here, please."

"I didn't order anything."

"Are you Andrew O'Hanlon?" Andy nodded. "Says here you did."

"Who is it from?"

"Listen, guy, I just deliver them. Do you want it or not?"

Protocol dictated he should not accept packages until they were checked out by the hazard team but he could not think anyone seeking him harm would know he was here; so he relented. As soon as he signed, the man stepped out of sight of the door and returned with a package on a dolly. He brought it into the room and made no pretense that he wasn't waiting for a tip. Andy was intrigued and handed the man the first thing he pulled out of his pocket. The delivery man quickly pocketed the fifty and closed the door behind him as he left. Andy walked around the box slowly, looking for clues as to its origin. There were no markings except his name with address and name of the hotel.

Finally he thought, *What the heck!* and began clawing at the tape securing the top of the box. Once opened, he gingerly began pulling out the tissue paper as he chastised himself. "This is a bad, bad idea," he said aloud.

His body jolted when he saw a hand. He stood completely still. When the hand moved, he stepped back and drew his service revolver, pointing it at the opening. "Come out of there. Hands where I can see them."

He saw shapely hands and well-toned lovely arms, and then his heart stopped. Judy stood up and looked at him under her lashes. He couldn't move. He reminded himself to breathe.

"Andy, could you point that somewhere else?'

He came to himself with a start and holstered his weapon. He began tearing into the box to get to her. "I don't care why you are here. Don't say anything. Just let me touch you."

Judy laughed and began helping him tear away the barrier between them. She finally pushed through the last vestiges of the box and went into his arms. He simply held her. She felt the steady beat of his heart and never knew she could feel that good. They stood that way for several moments.

"Can I say something now?" she asked.

"Only if it's good."

"I don't hate you."

Andy chuckled. "Well, that's good." He pulled back to look at her face. "Why are you here?" He hoped he was strong enough for the answer.

"Because I want to be with you."

"Are you sure?"

"Well, I just FedExed myself to you. I think I'm pretty sure."

He laughed from glee and joy and disbelief, all rolled in one. Twirling her around, they both laughed like children. She thought, *Who knew she could feel this free.*

"Wow, I haven't thought past the rejection."

"Well, you better be thinking. I didn't come this far to be shown the door now."

"Oh, baby, you are not going anywhere." He framed her face with his hands. "I have thought about *this.*" He captured her lips with his.

She was able to respond to him with all the abandon that had been missing in her life. She had been sexually assaulted at seventeen and had shut herself off from men ever since. She knew, without a doubt, she was breaking free of that demon. It felt glorious.

Pouring all that pent-up passion into her kiss, she made Andy forget any other woman he had ever been with. He was branded now. A goner. And he loved it.

Kenann did not waste any time reaching out. Danny Mac had taught Granny how to Skype. She took one look at Kenann's face and said, "Talk to me." And she did. Granny listened intently, only interrupting for succinct questions. When Kenann had told her everything, she sat back and gave Granny a questioning look.

"This is not good, Kenann."

"That's all you got?"

Granny laughed. "No, smart aleck! This is very important information. Danny needs to know."

"What? That I'm crazy?"

"You are not crazy, dear. You are being used."

"Used?"

"You have never had these issues or symptoms before. You are not crazy."

"But, Granny, I am afraid that I am having a traumatic reaction."

"Does that make you crazy?" Granny gave her a very pointed look.

Kenann dropped her head. "I knew talking to you would help me. Of course it doesn't, and I have been very silly."

"That being said, dear, I am not sure this is coming from some trauma reaction."

"You don't?"

"No, you are being stalked."

"By the society?"

"Yes, and it is time to talk to Danny."

"Okay, Granny. Thank you for being my voice of reason."

"Take back your life, Kenann. You are a smart cookie. Don't allow yourself to be a victim."

Kenann could feel her shoulders and spine straightening. She grabbed her phone and called Danny Mac. When he answered, she said, "Danny Mac, I am calling a council of war."

6

DANNY MAC AND Kenann made their way up the long tree-shaded drive to Mrs. Gage's large Gothic home holding hands. They had spent the last two days talking, knowing their lives were about to change *again.* It had taken that long to get everyone in place for the meeting. Mrs. Gage owned one of the largest homes (estates, really) in Memphis. As they started up the wide stone steps leading to the platform landing, the front door opened to reveal a diminutive woman with frosted hair and a large personality.

"There you are, my sweets. Everyone is gathered in the parlor. Oh, I have missed you two."

"Hello, Mrs. Gage." Danny Mac took her hands in his and kissed her on the cheek.

She leaned into Kenann for another kiss. Kenann was comforted by the scent of her signature perfume. Mrs. Gage turned and led them into the massive foyer and to the right into the parlor. The people sitting around the fireplace looked like a family gathering—comfortable and relaxed together. Jake Taylor, a large grizzled man, who had commanded Danny Mac in battle, had their ten-year-old mascot Blade in a headlock and was tickling him in the ribs while Judy and Andy looked on laughing. Mrs. James, Kenann's grandmother entered from the side patio door where she had been enjoying the garden.

"Granny!" Kenann ran and wrapped her arms around her. "When did you get here and why didn't you tell me you were coming?"

"I'm just full of surprises." She reached out a hand for Danny Mac, who obliged her by wrapping his arms around his two favorite women. It was then that they were struck by the scene of Andy with his arm around Judy, who was nestled in next to him.

"Well, well!" Kenann beamed. "It seems we have a development." Judy's smile was magnificent as she turned and looked up at Andy. He looked down at her as if she were the only person in the room or in the world. Danny Mac broke the spell by coming behind them and inserting his face between them for a hug. "It's about time. I was afraid I was going to have to hire Angelo to kidnap one of you to get this ball rolling."

The silence was deafening. Danny Mac looked up, afraid his humor had missed the mark, when suddenly, the room erupted in laughter. Relieved, he joined in and grabbing Kenann's hand, pulled her down to sit with him in the oversized chair next to the fireplace.

Mrs. Gage was firmly ensconced as the unofficial leader of this merry band of misfits and stood at the focal point in front of the group. "Kenann has called this council of war. We have been home for a few weeks now, and I think it is time we process our experiences both individually and collectively. First I must ask if anyone feels anything particularly pressing."

No one spoke for several moments. Jake cleared his throat and straightened his posture. "Gabrielle, you know my thoughts but I will discuss it for the benefit of the group. I have been deeply troubled by what we have found to be the scope of this society we uncovered. I have had a very hard time wrapping my mind around this and making sense of it. To be honest, I am angry and perplexed that this could have been allowed to go on for apparently thousands of years." He paused. "And as much as I am loath to admit, it has shaken my faith somewhat. I have so many questions. I know we need not ask why, but I do." He leaned back as if spent.

Granny James nodded several times, deep in thought. "Jake, I have to admit some of the same feelings. I know God is still in control, but it does shake me a bit. Andy, have they learned anything new?"

All eyes turned to Andy. He shook his head. "Carter has been working nonstop on the intel coming in. I told him I needed some personal time." He glanced down at Judy and smiled. "He was so caught up in it all he just grunted and waved me away. I took that as permission and took the next flight to Memphis. He sent me a message this morning to get my ass back to DC and bring all of you with me. I had planned to save that little bit for later."

Danny Mac became more alert. He maintained a healthy sense of guardedness where governmental authority was concerned. "Andy, he already offered Kenann a job, which she declined. What does he want?"

"Danny, you know he doesn't respond to the word *no*. He has been given the directive to take point on this task force. He is caught in the competition between us, Mossad, and MI6. He needs us."

"All of us?" Blade asked expectantly.

Andy smiled indulgently. "Yes, you have proven to be a trustworthy soldier and have more than earned a place on this team."

Blade became solemn as he absorbed this praise. He knew his mom would kill him if he joined any more trips like the last one by stowing away on Mrs. Gage's plane. His mom was grateful for

Danny Mac's help since his father's death last year from sickle-cell anemia; but Blade knew he wouldn't be doing that again.

Mrs. Gage spoke up. "Andy, can you tell us exactly why Carter needs us?"

"Even though the computer information we retrieved from the underground facility was extensive as well as the information Angelo provided, the organization has been able to cover their tracks well. It appears to be the key as to how they have survived this long. They had contingencies in place that allowed them to disappear and go underground without a trace."

Jake offered, "That explains the disappearance of the state department official you recognized in the crowd that night."

"Exactly," Andy agreed. "Gone, along with any paper or electronic trace of his activity while in office. It is an ingenious system, comprehensive. Even though his disappearance hit the news, there has been no hint of his involvement in a secret society."

Danny Mac persisted, "Why all of us, Andy?"

"Because we are Carter's bargaining chip to stay in command. No one else got closer to the core of this society; and as long as Carter has us under his command, he can run the show. Otherwise, he is just another analyst."

Danny Mac added, "We are going to have to discuss this as a group and weigh all the ramifications of teaming up with Carter. I sold my soul to him once. I don't plan on doing it again."

Mrs. Gage turned to Kenann. "Dear, you have said nothing, and it was you who asked to have this meeting."

Kenann looked around at the people who had all risked their lives for her. She was afraid to her very marrow. She felt the minute she spoke, things would be put in motion and there would be no going back. She took a very deep breath, letting it out slowly. All eyes looked at her with love. She dove in. "I am counting on your understanding and plead with you not to overreact, okay?" She waited until they all agreed verbally or by gesture. "Something strange has been happening. I don't have the answers. All I can do is tell you what it is. I am not crazy; and I really don't think it is a result of the trauma from this summer." She winked at Granny in silent thanks for her clear reasoning. No one moved a muscle but continued to look at her intently.

"Okay," she forged on. "I have been seeing shadows when I look out the window, and sometimes think I see someone standing at the edge of the woods. They are wearing those brown robes like what we saw in the underground cavern. The hoods are pulled down over their faces so I cannot see who it is. I have run downstairs to confront them, but they disappeared. And I also dream dreams that shake me up, and I black out. The other night, Danny Mac found me out cold in the backyard."

Everyone looked to Danny Mac for confirmation. He added, "I had entertained the idea that Pierre hypnotized her at some point. She definitely went off-the-book on the platform in Egypt. That would explain a lot of this. That means someone is getting close enough to administer whatever trigger Pierre set up. If it hadn't been for a large yellow dog barking and growling that woke me up, they might have had her. As soon as I came out and saw Kenann on the ground, the dog ran away. It may have saved her life."

Kenann pressed on. "And I am hearing things, chanting or sometimes screaming. It unnerves me. I haven't said anything before now because I was afraid I was going crazy. Then I got mad. I am *not* crazy. I want to get to the bottom of this."

Mrs. Gage reached over and put her hand over Kenann's hand.

"Dear, we *will* get to the bottom of this, most assuredly. Any ideas?" She looked around the room.

Judy was the only one with enough confidence to ask. "Kenann, are you sure these aren't hallucinations?"

"Well, of course I can't be 100% sure on something like that, but my gut says they aren't. Now the voices, I suppose, could be, but they sure don't seem like it. And I never hear them when anyone else is around. That's suspicious. If they were hallucinations, they would come indiscriminately."

Andy turned to Danny for confirmation. "Have you heard anything?"

"No, but I believe Kenann. I knew something was bothering her, but she is not losing touch with reality. If she were, wouldn't there be other subtle signs?"

"Hello? Crazy person still in the room!" Everyone laughed. "Clinically, you are right, Danny Mac. Someone who is hallucinating or becoming delusional will often show some deterioration in other areas. Social skills, hygiene, stuff like that."

Jake offered, "Well, then that leaves the option that there is someone stalking Kenann from that cult."

"If they are making contact in this way, we can use it," Andy interjected.

Judy glared up at him. He held her gaze. She spat, "So you are willing to use her again for your means."

"Yes, I am. Kenann is a tough cookie. Carter would never have offered her a job if he didn't think she could handle it. This may be an opportunity we cannot afford to pass up."

Judy searched every face in the room to find reinforcement that this idea was wrong. She found none. Even Kenann looked resigned.

"Judy, I know why you feel that way and I appreciate it, but Andy is right. I didn't choose to still be involved in this, but apparently, I am. It is what it is, and we have to play the hand we are dealt."

"Well, it still stinks. And you, mister,"—her glare was a little softer—"are in charge to make sure that nothing happens to my best friend."

"That's *my* job, Judy." Danny Mac looked deadly serious.

Kenann rolled her eyes. "Honestly, Danny Mac, I'm not helpless."

He captured her chin with his hand and looked intently in the eyes. "I am *going* to take care of you. Deal with it."

At that moment, a butler in full livery appeared at the door to the parlor. Kenann was once again reminded that Mrs. Gage lived in a whole different world than her. "Madame, a gentleman wishes to join your company."

"Who is it, Dawson?"

"He says his name is Carter." The entire room stirred in unison.

"Show him in and implement the increased security measures, please."

"Yes, Madame."

7

ALL EYES FACED the doorway as Carter, a section chief of the CIA, entered the room. He was a compact man who made up what he lacked in stature with his commanding demeanor. He wasted no time.

"I see I have come at a fortuitous time. Finding all of you together saves me time. The only person we are missing is Angelo. I know you know where he is, Danny. I need you to get him here. Pronto."

He did not wait for a reply, self-assured that his orders would be carried out. Kenann felt Danny Mac stiffen beside her. Carter forged on. "We are nearing completion of our analysis of the records we retrieved from the underground facility in the desert of Egypt. That and the information Danny provided on the scrolls he reviewed at Monforte's villa have painted a very disturbing picture. Of course, the scrolls were gone by the time we got to the villa, but thankfully for us, you have an almost perfect recollection. I have left you alone for the last few weeks while our analysts completed their work. No more. I need to pull out every memory, every last nuance you remember to get a handle on this bunch. They aren't done. And like a wounded animal, I fear we have only made them more dangerous."

Mrs. Gage took back her command of the room. "Mr. Carter, it is a delight to have you with us, and we do appreciate you leaving us alone." Carter zoomed in on her. Andy dropped his gaze to hide his smile. "And we have much to tell you. If you will make yourself comfortable, we will do our best to bring you up to speed."

Carter had no choice but to sit. He looked at Andy and sneered, "Personal business, huh?"

Andy's fair complexion betrayed him. Judy stuck out her chin, daring him to say another word. Carter secretly admired her spunk and made a tactical retreat.

Mrs. Gage nodded to Danny Mac. "Will you be so kind?"

He rose from his seat and stood a little apart to address Carter. He related the apparent harassment of Kenann by these forces, what she was hearing and seeing. He acknowledged Carter's assessment that this secret society continued to be a considerable threat and went on to say he felt they were planning to target Kenann. And for that reason alone, he would do everything within his power to stop this cabal. Then Danny turned to Kenann. She raised an eyebrow seeing something in his eyes but remained silent. "Kenann has expressed for several weeks that we should wait to marry."

"Danny Mac!" Kenann drew out his name in exasperation.

"Not one word till I am finished." She crossed her arms and pursed her lips in a perfect pout. "I have tried to be patient and wait her out but in light of this news, I am calling on all of your assistance to reason with her. I need to be with her. I *need* to protect her."

No one said a word for several moments, unsure what to say or do. Granny James stood slowly and walked over to Kenann and sat where Danny Mac had vacated. Granny took her hands, and Kenann looked at her, tears beginning to brim her eyes.

"Granny," was all she said.

"Sweetheart, I have watched you grow up. I have seen you close yourself off from emotional pain in order to survive the gypsy lifestyle your parents created for you."

Kenann's parents worked for the National Geographic Society and died in a plane crash earlier that year. Kenann was home-schooled all over the world growing up. She never put down roots or allowed herself the luxury of becoming emotionally involved with anyone.

Granny James continued. "I know you love Danny Mac, and I also know you can trust him." She looked up and met Danny Mac's eyes before returning her gaze to Kenann. "There is no reason to shut him out. I know you are scared of this next step because you have never allowed yourself to be vulnerable. He will protect even that, dear. Let's do this, honey."

Kenann looked down for several moments. No one breathed. She looked up and met Danny Mac's eyes. "Okay."

He asked, "Really?"

"Yeah, really."

Everyone was on their feet, talking at once. Carter, forgotten, sat glaring in confusion at the activity surrounding him. Danny Mac and Kenann were in their own bubble at that moment, oblivious to the chaos in the room.

Danny Mac whispered, "Are you sure, Kenann? I know I strong-armed this."

"Oh, Danny Mac! I've been silly. Granny is right, I am just scared. I refuse to be ruled by fear anymore. We will meet our life head on—whatever it holds—together."

He brought her fingers to his lips. "I love you."

Andy looked at Judy. "Does this give you any ideas?'

"If that's a proposal, you're going to have to do better than that, buddy."

8

THE GIRLS WERE congregated upstairs at Mrs. Gage's house in a cozy room none of them had seen before. Kenann wondered if Mrs. Gage herself has seen all the rooms in this monstrous house.

Mrs. Gage had herded them out shortly after Kenann had agreed to marry Danny Mac. "Kenann, dear, I am so relieved and happy you have made this decision."

"Relieved?"

"Well, perhaps not the best choice of words, but it concerned me that you would succumb to fear and thwart any effort at this happiness. And to be honest, I agree with Danny Mac. You need to be protected."

"Yes, sweetheart," Granny James placed her small hand over Kenann's. "I think there is something evil after you. You need someone strong who can protect you in the earthly realm and a spiritual warrior to defend you in the celestial realm. Danny Mac is both of those."

"Granny, do you honestly believe I am being attacked by something demonic?"

"You may find it hard to believe but, in a word, yes."

Mrs. Gage weighed in. "I do not begin to understand the spiritual aspects the way Moira or Danny Mac do, but I have been around the world several times and have seen things that defy any earthly or physical explanation. So I am inclined to agree that the possibility exists. If their own press is to be believed, this society has wielded a lot of power through the millennia."

"The Bible itself says that the ancient gods and goddesses that were worshipped were actually demons," Granny James added. "I think we need to be alert on all fronts."

Judy was just listening until now. "Okay, we may have to battle the forces of evil, but right now, we have a wedding to plan."

"Yes!" was the unanimous chorus. Kenann giggled.

The boys remained downstairs in the den. After the usual backslapping and congratulations for finally wearing Kenann down, they got down to business.

Carter made perfunctory congratulatory remarks and then asked Danny Mac, "What do you make of the things Kenann told you?"

"I knew something was off with her and couldn't put my finger on it, but I kept reminding myself she killed a person. The big question now is who or what is doing these things to her because I know something is actually happening."

"I can guarantee it is." All eyes turned to Carter. He went on. "I didn't want to say too much in front of the women."

Andy laughed and said, "You'd better not let them catch you saying that."

Jake chimed in and winked at Andy. "Full and equal partners. Gabrielle will have your hide."

Carter did not appear to see the humor. Danny Mac was very quiet too as he waited to hear what he had to tell them. "There have been multiple killings recently across the globe. That is what brought me here today. They appear too random for the major news agencies to pick them up, but they are all people on our short list to talk with about this society. They are tying up loose ends and you folks are definitely loose ends to them."

Danny Mac asked, "Do you think they are planning something big?"

"No, I think they probably were, but they're on the defensive now. Their sole objective is the preservation of their order. I just wish I knew what they were all about." Carter paused and looked at Danny Mac. "Kenann is the key, you know that, don't you?"

"Yes."

"Are you willing to let me use that…her to bring them down?"

"Only if you use me to protect her."

"Could I stop you?"

"No."

"Then let's work together. She won't be safe till this bunch is brought down. None of you will be, for that matter."

"What's the plan?" Jake asked.

"I am counting on Danny to help me out with that."

Danny Mac simply looked at Carter. He appeared to already be working on that plan in his head. Andy had been watching Danny Mac closely as he talked, thinking about all the times Danny had led them as team leader in the Marine Corps. It felt good to be here with him again, even though Danny chafed at the idea of being back in this business.

Carter suggested, "Call Angelo."

"David," Danny Mac reminded him absently. He remained lost in his own thoughts.

"Well, whatever you call him now, he may be the only one who can pinpoint who is leading the group now. We need to jog his memory some more."

Danny Mac added, "With Katarina and Pierre out of the picture, I cannot think who would want to target Kenann in particular. All of us were culpable for the discovery of this society."

"Kenann was considered to be fulfillment of prophecy, right?" Carter asked.

"By Pierre. I can't say by anyone else. It seemed most of the people around him were simply indulging his fantasy. But to be honest, most of the ones I met were simply his muscle."

"Someone must have believed in Pierre or he would not have risen to the top of this society. If he thought she was Inanna, it's possible others continue to believe it. We have no way to know with whom he communicated about his belief in Kenann. But one thing seems pretty certain, someone is intent on getting their hands on her for some reason."

"Over my dead body," Danny Mac's voice was ice cold.

"Until this is over, all of you are getting a security detail, and for goodness' sake, get that girl wedded and bedded so we can get on with this."

He did not see the look of irritation on Danny Mac's face.

9

Since everyone Kenann or Danny Mac cared about was right there, he told her there was no reason to wait. He also didn't want to give her time to change her mind. She did, occasionally, resemble a deer in headlights but clamped down on her fears with the help of Granny.

They met all the requirements of the state of Tennessee. Jake had his license to perform marriage ceremonies. The only thing left was the finery. Mrs. Gage had this well in hand. She orchestrated this the same way Patton marched the Third Army through Germany. All the men were fitted with tuxedos. Once Kenann mentioned her favorite colors were mauve and navy blue, the flowers and decorations were obtained in short order. All that remained were gowns. This required some time for the ladies to thoroughly enjoy the experience. They were going to have their day. Mrs. Gage insisted on taking care of all costs, saying she had more money than she could spend in two lifetimes and she was going to spend it the way she wanted. No arguments.

The night before the grand excursion, Kenann thought she heard something on the front porch. She went into the main hall; and with the ever-present security watching out for her, she had no qualms about opening the front door. Looking up at her was a huge yellow dog. He was bigger than a golden retriever but had the look of one with a strong handsome face. They simply stood staring at each other for several moments. Then the dog dropped his head, trotted into the foyer, and turned into the open door to her apartment.

Kenann stood amused, looking after him. "Well, make yourself at home, buddy."

She followed him into the room. The dog was standing in the middle of the floor, watching her as if waiting for a command. "Don't you look rough and ready." The dog wagged his tail; she was smitten. "Okay, Rough, we have to lay down some ground rules. I am getting married this weekend. There will be no sleeping in my bed. Well, not for a while. Are you housebroken?"

He barked. "I'll take that as a yes."

Danny Mac came through the door. "Hey, that's the dog."

"Yes, his name is Rough, and he has adopted me."

"Hello, Rough. No sleeping in our bed."

"We have already discussed that. He tells me he is housebroken."

"That's good. What does he eat?"

"No clue."

Danny Mac walked over and ruffled the dog's head. "You're a big guy, aren't you? Where did you come from? Well, no matter. You looked out for Kenann so you are golden."

"No pun intended?" Kenann laughed.

"Yeah, he's a golden retriever on steroids. Why are you calling him *Rough*?"

"It's short for *rough and ready*."

She dropped to her knees and put her arms around his neck, nuzzling him. His tail drummed a tattoo on the back of the couch. She looked up at Danny Mac and smiled. His heart skipped a beat. He could not remember existing before she came into his life.

Kenann saw the look of love come over Danny Mac as he looked down at her; she knew she was making the right decision at the right time.

"Look, Danny Mac, we have started our little family."

He dropped to his knees. He wasn't sure they would hold him. He put his hand on Rough's back to steady himself. "We haven't really talked about kids."

Kenann burst out laughing. "Look at the big bad Marine scared out of his wits. Down, tiger. I wasn't suggesting kids."

"Well, don't you want any?" Now he felt defensive.

"I don't know. I wasn't planning on getting married so the whole kid thing has never been on my radar. What do you want?"

"Well, I guess I am the same as you. Looks like we both have some thinking to do."

Hoping bravado would help distract her from her fears, she gave Danny Mac a wicked grin and said, "I can't think past the honeymoon."

10

THE WOMEN MET at Mrs. Gage's estate for high tea before leaving to go to the wedding boutique. She outfitted each of them with a special hat from her own wardrobe to complement their outfits and they "retired to the veranda" to be served tea and biscuits. They giggled like children playing dress up and compared notes on their respective bodyguards.

Mrs. Gage seemed more relaxed than any had seen her as she talked about some of her adventures over the years. No one interrupted beyond trying to encourage her to continue. She told them of the death of her first love fighting the Soviets in Hungary. It was at this time when she met her husband. Mr. Gage was the origin of her current wealth. She was young and spirited. He was several years her senior and very charming. What she did not know then was his charm masked a darker sadistic side. He gloried in subjugating her in private. In public, he was the epitome of deference and consideration; in private, he laughed at her tears and made her beg for even the slightest kindness. She never knew why she stayed. It was not for the money. It meant nothing to her then; and even now, it was simply a means to other ends. She believed in keeping promises when she had made a vow before God. It was probably as simple as that.

When he died after five years of marriage, she felt defeated. She had never been able to get him to love her. As the final insult, she found out from his lawyer he had been in the process of writing her out of his will. Since it was not finalized when he dropped dead on the golf course, she inherited it all. It took her a year or two to recover. When she finally regained her sense of self, she vowed she would never let someone control or affect her that way again. Looking back, she did not think she ever loved him; but she was desperate to belong to someone or something. She eventually found her meaning in helping others in ways no one else could or would. It was during these years she honed her craft and developed a network of resources that enable her to impact peoples' lives on a global scale. When Kenann jokingly called her an International Woman of Mystery, she had no idea how close to the truth it was. Mrs. Gage revealed none of this, except to recount funny or poignant episodes that dotted her history. She had them all laughing and shaking their head at her chutzpah.

At one point, Granny James reached over and laid her hand over Mrs. Gage's. "Gabrielle, you are a wonderful woman who deserves everything you give to others. When are you going to let Jake into your life on a permanent basis?"

"Oooh, Mrs. Gage. We could make it a double ring ceremony?" Judy laughed.

Mrs. Gage deflected, "Or a triple!"

Judy blushed and Kenann jumped on this as Mrs. Gage knew she would. Granny James gave Mrs. Gage a knowing look. Mrs. Gage responded with the slightest of shrugs.

Kenann slapped Judy on the shoulder. "What's the dish, Crawford? You and the strapping G-Man going to make it official?"

"One shotgun wedding at a time, if you please."

"Hey, what do you mean? This is not a shotgun wedding."

"Oh please! If you don't go down that aisle, Danny Mac is coming after you with both barrels!"

Mrs. Gage clapped her hands after the laughter subsided. "Come on ladies, let's go paint the town."

The women had the time of their lives. They had never laughed so much or felt so carefree. It may have been a conscious effort in light of the troubles that lie ahead. Regardless, they had fun. They came back to Mrs. Gage's estate loaded with parcels and bags. Kenann and Danny Mac had decided to marry at Mrs. Gage's house so the women laid out everything they needed for the next day's events.

"Well, my dears, we have had a banner day. What say ye now?"

Judy spoke up. "We could have a slumber party?" Kenann was amazed at the change in Judy.

"Excellent idea! Moira, Kenann, are you in favor?"

Both agreed so she dispatched everyone back to their homes (with security detail in tow) to fetch pajamas and bring their junk food of choice. Granny James and Kenann were laughing as they entered the foyer. Both stopped dead in their tracks and then began forcibly jockeying for the front position in order to protect each other. They had almost wrestled to the floor when Danny Mac came in behind them. He put both of them bodily outside on the porch while he and Rough began securing the area.

It was a mess. Things were pulled off walls and shelves and strewn all over the floor. The most disturbing sight was the word *whore* written in what looked like blood splatter on the large window at the top of the stairway landing. Kenann and Granny James stood in the doorway, watching the stealth and control with which Rough and Danny Mac worked together. No one made a sound until they came back down the stairs and walked out on the porch, joining the women and their bodyguards.

"What do you make of this, Danny Mac?" Granny James asked.

"It wasn't a robbery. To be honest, it looks like someone had a huge temper tantrum."

"You think?" Kenann said sarcastically.

"Kenann, we cannot let them get to us. We are going through with our plans." She did not look convinced but nodded anyway. Granny James took her by the arm.

"Danny Mac will have to call the police and deal with all of that." Granny James looked at him, "I'm sure he will also call Andy." Danny Mac nodded. "Let's get our things and go back to Gabrielle's. Danny Mac and Andy can come later and let us know what they find. All right?" Kenann nodded again and allowed herself to be led up the stairs past the blood spatter.

Rough looked up to Danny Mac who sensed his attention. He looked down. "I know, boy, I'm worried too."

11

Andy and Danny Mac stood in the foyer, watching the local law enforcement leave in their vehicles. Andy thought they did a decent job with their investigation. Neither he nor Danny Mac volunteered any information regarding who they knew to be the perps. This one will go down as unsolved as far as the Memphis police would ever know. The two men standing shoulder to shoulder would now take care of this—guaranteed.

Danny Mac spoke quietly. "I found out how they were tormenting Kenann with voices and screams."

"Really? How?"

He produced two small transmitter/receivers from his pants pocket. "I found these in Kenann's bedroom and bath during my sweep earlier."

Andy added, "And producing the trigger set up by Pierre to bring on the trance."

"I'm slipping, Andy. I should have looked for these as soon as she told me what was happening."

Andy looked at Danny Mac and saw the burden he carried to keep Kenann safe.

Surveying the damage, he said, "I will not see that look on Kenann's face again. As soon as we are back from our honeymoon, we are going after these people."

"What do you mean back from your honeymoon? You seriously aren't considering going off on your own?"

"Well, I'm not taking you on my honeymoon. But I might as well. I've got a whole contingency assigned by Carter. It is worth it for the simple fact that Carter is not getting his way on this. He wanted me to forget the honeymoon."

"Where are you going?"

"Jake's cabin in the Ozarks."

Andy threw his hands in the air and turned in a circle. "Could you find anyplace more remote? Jeez, Danny!"

"Jake has made sure there is firepower in the cabin. We will be fine. If anyone gets by Carter's ring of steel, they'll have to come through me to get to Kenann."

"Well, at least let me create a diversion."

"Go for it, but run it by Carter first. I promised no going rogue."

"What do you and Carter have cooked up?"

"We may take this group on a merry chase."

"Expound."

"I want to take advantage of having them on the defensive. We have started here and are building a profile of anything suspicious in Memphis, anything that doesn't fit. Then we are going to take our show on the road. We will send in a forward team to do some recon. We will build a profile based on changes in the local chatter or behavior. In this way, they will hopefully give us a tell. Angelo…David," he corrected himself, "will be here tomorrow. This group sees us as the *team* that put them on the run. And this is the team that is going to hunt them down."

They picked up Jake and filled him in on the way. He reminded Danny Mac that even though he was more than welcome to use the cabin, he was relieved that there would be security on site and that they were being led by Johnson and Whitaker, who had been with Andy in Egypt. Andy checked the cell service and breathed easier knowing that a strong signal was available there. He transferred the men's cell numbers to Danny Mac. He asked Danny Mac to text them to check in. That would be the extent of their intrusion on his and Kenann's honeymoon, Andy promised. Danny Mac pinned him with his gaze. "I promise!" he protested.

Danny Mac's look said it all. Andy made a mental note to threaten his men with court martial if they made their presence known to Kenann in any way. It was late by the time the men made it to Mrs. Gage's. They were let into the parlor. A few minutes later, the women filed in, dressed in robes and slippers. The men collectively grinned at them.

"Aren't you all cute," Andy said. He was given a look from *she who must be obeyed*. He raised his hands in supplication and mouthed to Judy, "What?" Judy just grinned back at him; her eyes never left his face.

"Gentlemen, report please." Mrs. Gage was all business despite her attire. Kenann's eyes still looked bruised on her pale face while Granny wore the look of a warrior.

Danny Mac took over. "As anticipated, there were no identifiers left behind, but I did find the transmitters they used to convince you that you were hearing voices." Kenann nodded and stared at the devices in Danny Mac's hand. Danny Mac continued, "The police did a nice job going over the scene and agreed to contact Andy if they come up with anything while Kenann and I are away."

"Away?" The women spoke as one. Kenann only looked at Danny Mac with relief and love. He had guessed right. It was exactly what she needed.

Andy rescued him. "It will be fine. We have taken precautions. For once, Mrs. Gage, you will have to trust us to handle this."

"I am not accustomed to relying on anyone but myself."

Jake mumbled, "Tell me about it."

Mrs. Gage gave him a withering look but said nothing. "Very well then, Kenann, are you comfortable with this?"

Kenann never took her eyes from Danny Mac and whispered, "Yes." Danny Mac winked at her and her heart did a monumental flip and dropped to her feet.

Danny Mac turned to the others in the room. "I told Andy to make sure Carter is ready as soon as we are back. I also told him we would all be available to him." No one spoke. Their mutual determination was evident. Then he added, "This has to end."

12

THE DAY DAWNED cool and crisp for September in Memphis. The ceremony was set for 12:30 p.m. with reception following. Danny Mac and Andy picked Angelo up at the airport that morning. Danny Mac gave him a suit to wear and asked Angelo to be part of the security detail. Johnson, Whitaker, and other agents donned their suits and were good at blending in as the guests arrived.

Upstairs, Kenann sat quietly with Granny as she was looking out the window. Granny was concerned at Kenann's lack of obvious nerves. "What are you thinking, honey?"

"Oh, just what it would be like if Mom and Dad were here. Wonder if they would have made time to come?"

"They didn't do right by you, and I'm not proud to admit it. We both know they did the best they were capable of."

"They probably should never have had kids, huh, Granny?"

"But I thank God every day that they did."

Kenann went into Granny's arms. She did not cry. She simply wanted the comfort. "You have always been my center, Granny."

"Now you have Danny Mac for that."

"What if I disappoint him? What if he decides he made a mistake?"

"Oh dear! I am not going to make empty promises. Marriage is hard work and there will be bumps, but you two are determined and stubborn enough to work them out. He adores you, Kenann. He is not infatuated with you. He truly needs you. Open yourself to what he is offering and believe a little bit in yourself, kid."

Kenann sighed. "Wow! Big day, huh?"

"Yes, it is. One of the biggest and I'm so glad I am here to see it happen."

Kenann took a deep breath and stood up. She held out her hand to Granny and said, "Let's get this party started."

Mrs. Gage and Judy were waiting in the adjoining room. They all admired each other and their choice of colors and gowns. Mrs. Gage and Granny were in the same midnight-blue dress but in different styles. Judy was gorgeous with her hair swept up and a strapless gown of softly draped mauve material that complimented her skin tone perfectly.

They encircled Kenann to inspect and admire her. The gown was simple and draped in soft folds to the floor. The cap sleeves and heart-shaped bodice was adorned with small pearls. Her headpiece fit closely and was adorned with identical small pearls. Her veil had been altered at the last minute by executive decision. It was opaque and covered her face and hair. Andy had a plan.

They all heard the music begin and joined hands in their circle. As always, Mrs. Gage rallied her troops. "Kenann, we are all honored to share this day with you. You are a part of our hearts and our lives. And don't ever forget, we've got your back."

Kenann laughed. "You guys are the best. Who wouldn't be the happiest girl in the world with what I have here and what is waiting for me down there?"

Judy cheered, "Go team!"

Everyone laughed. Holding hands, they walked down the wide gothic stairs side by side and into the ballroom that was laid out for the reception to follow. Blade was waiting there, looking handsome in his tuxedo and holding the open Bible where their two rings laid on. The ceremony was to be held outside in the garden. The audience made up entirely of people from their church family. Mrs. Gage waited for the appropriate musical cue and walked through the center French doors, across the patio, and down the stairs to the aisle between white chairs, leading to where Jake, Danny Mac and Andy waited. Jake winked at her. She smiled back and thought how tired she was of fighting her battles alone.

Andy beamed when he saw Judy come through the doors. Their eyes met and never wavered as she walked toward him. In their hearts, this marked a special time to celebrate their newfound love as well. Blade walked stiffly through to the patio, monitoring his sacred trust of the rings. He wasn't this nervous when they bound and placed him on the sacrificial slab in Egypt. Of course, he had always known Danny Mac would save him. This was all on him to get those rings down there without dropping them. *Almost there. One more step. Okay, now stand beside Jake where they told you. No time to practice. Done.* When he finally looked up, everyone was smiling. *Mission accomplished.* He blew out his breath, and Jake chuckled beside him.

The music swelled as Jake raised his hands to signal everyone to stand. Granny James and Kenann stepped out of the French doors and paused for the briefest of seconds. It was as if they both wanted to savor it before proceeding. In that moment, Danny Mac felt everyone and everything fade away. It was if he saw his life and his past with pure clarity, that he was meant to come here to this place, this day, and to this woman. Kenann's opaque veil did not hide her glow. She couldn't help it, she started laughing with delight. She could almost feel the bricks falling away from her emotional prison cell. At the sound of her laughter, others began to smile. It was infectious. By the time she reached Danny Mac, everyone was smiling or laughing and feeling pretty good about life.

They stopped in front of Jake who asked the traditional question, "Who gives this woman to be married?"

Granny lifted up Kenann's veil. Looking at her, she said, "I do." They smiled at each other. Granny took Kenann's hand and Danny Mac's hand and brought them together. Without another word, she took her place on the front row. Jake motioned for everyone to be seated.

Kenann and Danny Mac went through the motions answering all the questions and saying the vows; but they became truly united in the questions and answers they gave through their eyes.

You know I love you.

Yes, I do.

I will always be there for you.

I know, and you know what a nut I can be at times.

Yes, and that is one of the things I love about you. We are going to make it.

Yes, we will.

"May I now introduce to you Mr. and Mrs. Daniel MacKenzie. Daniel, you may now kiss your bride."

He smiled at her. She smiled back. His kiss was tender. Kenann, forgetting everyone but Danny Mac, felt herself begin to drift. When he raised his head, she swayed. Everyone broke into laughter. They turned around, and Danny Mac raised their joined hands in a sign of triumph. The watchers had not been able to penetrate the security to join this gathering, despite their leaders express demand. The crowd clapped as they went down the aisle to the veranda to greet their guests. They were joined by the rest of the wedding party. Leading the group was Granny and Blade arm in arm, followed by Judy and Andy, then Mrs. Gage and Jake. They stood in a circle of hands for a moment; each thinking similar thoughts. This bond had been forged through adversity; but it was thriving out of love, undying loyalty, and devotion to each other. They are family.

The reception was as lighthearted and fun as the ceremony. There was lots of food and libations. Johnson, Whitaker, and Angelo checked the perimeter frequently as well as inside the massive house. Mrs. Gage's subtle security was on the job as well.

Andy had devised a diversion for the first part of his plan to keep Kenann safe. Andy and Judy made the announcement that they were going to chauffeur the bride and groom to their honeymoon suite and went out to get the car. They then slipped in through a garage entrance and hurriedly switched clothes with Danny Mac and Kenann, who then entered the limousine with darkened windows and brought it around to wait at the front door. Andy and Judy completed their disguise with amazingly accurate wigs. The rest of the crew were given strict instructions to bombard them with rice as the "bride and groom" raced with their heads down to the waiting car. Once inside, they sped away to the cheers of the crowd. Both Andy and Danny Mac were watching for tails. None were obvious.

"Danny Mac" made his way through town to the Peabody, where Andy had a room. They said their goodbyes and best wishes from the confines of the car as they parked under the portico. The faux bride and groom exited and kept their heads down as they went into the lobby and caught the elevator being held by Andy's backup. He had called in help in case the ruse worked too well, and they came after him or Judy before they realized they had been duped.

Meanwhile, as soon as Andy and Judy were out of the car, Danny Mac sped away toward I-40 and their Ozark mountain honeymoon cottage. Neither spoke until they crossed the Mississippi River into Arkansas.

Kenann blew out a huge breath and laid her head back on the headrest. She asked, "Now what?"

"We stop in West Memphis and change vehicles, just in case."

"I sure hope our stuff made it into this car. Wonder how Andy and Judy are doing?"

"To your first question, I did it myself and to your second question, I would say they are doing fine. But, more importantly, I am saying that for the next week, no one exists except you and me." Kenann looked over and studied Danny Mac as he drove. He never took his eyes from the road when he asked, "What?"

"Oh, just looking at my husband. Saying that is going to take some getting used to."

"Just shut your mind off and relax. Don't overthink *us*. We are good together, and we will stay good together till death do us part. We might even have a little fun."

She leaned her head back and closed her eyes. "Okay, buddy. I tried to warn you, but you are so totally stuck now." She didn't see the grin that spread across his face.

The blood boiled in the veins of the man sitting behind a bank of monitor screens. He watched the bride and groom make their way into the elevator through the lens of the man behind the front desk. He willed his breathing to slow. His smile was chilling, feral. Revenge for the attack on the order would be sweet. But first, he would torment and torture.

13

ANDY COULDN'T RESIST and scooped Judy up in his arms as soon as he had his hotel door opened and carried her across the threshold. She giggled like a school girl. The thought went through her mind that she *never* giggles. Well, not until she met Andy. He tossed her on the bed and leaped beside her.

"This is giving me all kind of ideas, girlfriend."

"Do you realize how gay that sounds, calling me girlfriend?"

"Well, you are my girlfriend, aren't you?"

She faltered just a little then laughed. "Well, I guess I am."

"You guess?"

"I am." They lay side by side and grinned at each other. "Andy?"

"Hmmm?"

"I have issues."

"Who doesn't?"

She sat up and turned to him, the wedding dress rustling between them. "I'm not sure I can have sex with you."

He coughed and sat up himself. "Uh, I wasn't really going to… uh—"

"No, I don't mean right now. I mean, I am not sure if I ever can."

"Okayyy?" stretching the word out in question. He kept his face calm and as impassive as possible as he waited for her to elaborate.

She heaved a huge sigh as she looked down. *In for a penny, in for a pound, Granny James always said.* "My only experience was multiple rapes as a teenager, and I have never let myself get close to anyone until now."

He longed to reach out but was afraid to spook her. His mind scrambled for the right words—and fast. *This explained so much.* "Judy," he began. "There is nothing, nothing that we can't work through. I am"—he struggled desperately for the right word—"honored that I am your first."

"How can you say that?"

"Look, I *am* your first. Whatever happened was not of your doing. You were not involved. We can put it behind us."

"How do you know? What if I am…frigid?"

He almost laughed but caught himself. "Judy, have you frozen up when we kiss? Or when I hold you in my arms?"

"Well, no."

"Then when we make love. We will take it slow, as slow as you need, and we will be fine."

"Do you really think so?"

"Yes, I do…so do you want to fool around?" She laughed (which was his intent) but then he asked gently, "Want to talk about it?"

She looked at him for a brief moment and started, "I was part of a youth group at church. The preacher took some of us to Europe on a mission trip the summer after my senior year of high school. He found ways to get me alone several times that summer. He said he had *God-given needs.*" She choked on the last words and started to cry.

He didn't hesitate this time but pulled her into his arms. "I want his name."

"No, Andy. Leave it alone."

"I am going to kill him." She jerked back and saw how deadly serious he was. He repeated, "I want his name."

"He's already dead."

"Liar."

"Andy, I don't need you to complicate this whole thing by going psycho on me."

"Trust me, I am very clear."

"Andy, let it go. I should have done something when it happened. I know that. But I was sick and in shock. I never told anyone until this summer. I told Mrs. Gage and Jake. I knew I had to get it off my back if I was going to be any good to Kenann. That sick bastard may not be dead, but he had a massive stroke when I went to college and is in a nursing home. My only regret is he never paid for what he did."

"Well, maybe he did."

14

DANNY MAC PULLED into the truck stop in West Memphis, Arkansas. Kenann raised an eyebrow; Danny Mac just smiled.

"A little errand for Mrs. Gage."

"What's up?"

"She has an apparent compatriot who makes truck runs for her as needed. He travels all over the United States, and he *pays attention* to things for her. She wants him to do some recon for us."

"How can he possibly help us?"

"Like I said, he pays attention. One of the things he has been noticing is feelers to take people across our northern and southern borders without undue questions. He is supposed to be pulling into this lot right about now."

Kenann followed Danny Mac's gaze to a tanker truck pulling up to the pumps. A tall man with salt-and-pepper hair climbed down from the cab.

"Is he wearing a muff?"

Danny Mac laughed. "My guess is that would be Freddie, his cat."

About that time, the muffler wagged its tail. Danny Mac stepped out of the car and approached him. Kenann rolled down the window to hear.

"You must be CJ Baer."

"That'd be me." He shook Danny's offered hand. "What can I do for my favorite little lady?"

"She has asked me to give you this envelope of instructions and to ask you to take one of those special runs into Canada. Can you do that?"

"For Mrs. Gage? Anything. Does she want me to use my same way to communicate with her?"

"She told me to instruct you to use protocol *B*. Does that make sense to you?"

"Sure does. I will find out as much as I can about this nonsense and contact her."

"CJ, be careful. These people are very dangerous. Don't look too interested or get too nosey."

"Son, I've been working for Mrs. Gage for several years. She put me through my paces, her very own boot camp." He laughed at the memory. "She is a jewel, that's for sure."

"Well, all right then, and thank you for your help."

"Glad to do it. And if you all need me to do anything else, all you gotta do is ask. Now if you will excuse me, me and Freddie here are gonna get some grub."

Freddie's tail twitched at the mention of his name. CJ shook Danny's hand again and walked into the truck stop with the gray tabby cat draped around his neck.

Kenann gasped. "Did that cat just wink at me?"

Danny laughed. "I think it did."

He got back into the car. "One more stop to switch vehicles and we should be on our way."

"How many people does Mrs. Gage have on her payroll?"

"I would be afraid to guess. But I am glad she is on our side."

As Danny Mac pulled up to the cabin he ran a perimeter check. Seeing nothing, he parked the car and came around to open Kenann's door. She turned, put her feet on the gravel drive, and looked up at him. Their eyes locked for a few seconds, and then she grinned.

He grinned back. "Hello, Mrs. MacKenzie."

"Hello, Mr. MacKenzie."

He held out his hand. She took it and stood in front of him. He wrapped his arms around her and held her for several seconds then took her hand and led her to the cabin. They stepped up on the porch. He unlocked and opened the door with the key Jake had provided. Before she had a chance to protest, Danny Mac picked Kenann up in his arms and carried her in.

Despite all the trouble that lay behind and before them, Kenann's heart felt light, and she laughed. "This is perfect, Danny! Not a soul around for miles."

He hoped the men who were guarding them kept out of sight for the next week. He wanted Kenann to relax and get used to the idea of being married. He felt she was still skittish.

"I'll get our bags."

"Want help?"

"No, I've got it. Check the place out."

She went into the kitchen and started opening cabinets. She found them fully stocked, same with the fridge. She wondered if she had Jake to thank for all this. The bathroom was huge and more luxurious than she expected in a remote cabin. Across the hall was a small bedroom. She went farther down the hall and opened the door to find the master bedroom and bath. Her eyes were drawn to the king-size bed dominating the room along with the large spa tub in one corner.

"How do you like it?"

Kenann jumped. "It's good. Good. Do you want something to eat?"

She turned and went down the hall quickly to the kitchen. Danny Mac followed her, grinning. Deciding on chicken alfredo, they worked easily together while preparing the dish. He wanted desperately to kiss her; but he was biding his time. She was nervous. He could wait a little longer. Danny Mac slid the casserole dish into a warming oven and turned to Kenann. She was looking at him intently. He raised a questioning eyebrow.

Kenann said, "I need to talk to you."

"Am I in trouble already?"

She laughed. "No, silly. I just want to talk to you about something."

"Well, let's go over and talk about it." He led her to the couch and pulled her down beside him.

She moved slightly from his embrace so she could look him in the eyes. "Danny Mac, I have been doing a lot of thinking."

"So what else is new?"

She slapped his shoulder. "I'm serious."

"Okay, I'm all ears."

"Remember when we were in Alexandria and you talked to me about how to give myself to God and be a Christian."

"Yes," Danny Mac was suddenly acutely alert.

"Well, I have been thinking. I want to do that. I want to start our life together, being one in the Lord." He sat and held her gaze intently. She held her breath. Finally, she broke the silence. "Well, say something."

His voice was husky with emotion. "Kenann, that is the best gift you could have given me today or any day."

She went into his arms, and they clung to each other, both deep in their own thoughts. Again, she broke the silence. "Let's change our clothes so you can baptize me. 'See, here is water, what does hinder me from being baptized?' to quote from Acts 9."

"You've been studying." Danny Mac grinned.

"A little. Wanted to make sure I knew what I was getting myself into." She laughed.

"Go get changed. I need to absorb this good news."

As soon as she had gone into the bedroom, he pulled out his cell and sent a text to Johnson, alerting him they were going to the lake and to make sure everyone was out of sight. Then he prepared a fire to warm them afterward.

Kenann came out in sweats and T-shirt. "Come on, MacKenzie. Time's a-wastin'."

He laughed and went to change as well. They walked hand in hand down the hill to the water's edge. He felt her hand trembling slightly. "Are you okay?"

"Yep. Just a big moment, you know."

"Yes it is. Are you ready?" She nodded her head. He led her into the water and turned to face her, taking both hands in his. "Kenann, love of my life and precious to me, do you believe that Jesus Christ is the son of God?"

"I do."

"I am honored to baptize you into Christ and to all that it means through the name of the Father, the Son and the Holy Spirit."

She held her nose and closed her eyes. Just before he lowered her under the water, she thought she heard a guttural cry somewhere in her head.

He raised her up as both were laughing in pure joy. She leaped into his arms and he twirled her around in the water. They came out and ran into the cabin. They huddled together near the fire and laughed. It was a moment of pure joy for them both.

"I can't wait to tell Granny. She will be so happy. She never pushed, but I know she has wanted this for me."

"What made you decide, Kenann?"

"I don't know exactly. I really felt God's presence when we were in Alexandra. When I called out to him, he was there for me, you know?"

"Yes, I do."

"And when I had all those dark dreams and felt that evil presence at times, I knew I wanted God in my life—and that's who I wanted to be a part of, not the other. It's ugly and dark and yucky."

"God is love, honey. He is light and truth and peace."

"All the good stuff."

"Yep."

"He created other good stuff too." Kenann gave him a wicked grin.

Danny raised an eyebrow. "Like what?"

"Sex."

"Oh, baby! I thought you'd never ask."

15

KENANN WAS NUZZLED into the curve of Danny Mac's body. The sound she made was a sigh, a murmur, and a purr all rolled together. She could feel Danny Mac chuckling. She grinned at herself and thought she must be the luckiest girl in the whole world. She trailed her finger down his chiseled chest.

"Kenann MacKenzie. I like the sound of that, Mr. MacKenzie."

"So do I, Mrs. MacKenzie."

"And I'm starving," Kenann exclaimed.

"Did you work up an appetite?" Danny Mac couldn't resist teasing her.

Kenann sat bolt upright. "Casserole!"

Danny Mac sat up too. "What?" He was ready to do battle; but his mind couldn't process what she was saying.

"Casserole in the oven. We never got it out!"

"You are so right." He laughed. "Come on, let's go see how much damage we've done." He climbed out of bed and walked toward the kitchen without a thought. Kenann grabbed his T-shirt off the floor before she left the bedroom. Danny Mac already had the blackened dish in the sink and opened the window to let out some of the smoke and smell. He turned when she entered and grinned. "You look good in my shirt."

"We are a married couple." She was still trying to get used to the idea. "This is so weird."

Danny Mac pulled her to him. He couldn't get enough of her. "Well, weird is not my choice of words but I'll take it. I love you, kid."

"I love you." She snuggled under his chin. "Now feed me."

"Okay, how does an omelet sound?"

"Yummy. I'll mix the eggs together. You can chop the onions."

"Onions?"

"Yep. I distinctly remember the phrase *for better or for worse* in there somewhere."

"You're going to use that against me a lot, aren't you?"

"Yep." She added, "And Danny Mac?"

"Hmm?" He was grabbing a knife out of the drawer to cut the onions.

"Could you put on some clothes? You're distracting me."

He laughed and patted the top of her head on his way to the bedroom. He came back out in low-slung jeans, grinning at her. "Sweetheart, you're going to have to get used to me being naked."

She had quickly diced some onions and was finishing whisking the eggs together. "I know, I know, but give me a break! I spent twenty odd years saying no. It's going to take me awhile to get used to going all willy-nilly."

"Willy-nilly?" Danny Mac laughed out loud. It was infectious.

Kenann giggled and shrugged. "You know what I mean."

He came up behind her, placing his arms around her waist and pulling her tightly back against him. He began nibbling on her ear. "But think of all the fun we are going to have learning to get all willy-nilly."

She leaned her head back against him and sighed. "I am so happy, Danny Mac. I have made my peace with God, and I have you the rest of my life. It seems too good to be true."

He squeezed her and came around her to cook the omelets. "I know what you mean. I had given up thinking I would find *the one*. Before, it was all about *love 'em and leave 'em*." He glanced at Kenann sheepishly.

"It's okay. I know you have a past. Remember, I met one of them."

"Yeah, don't remind me. But when I came to the Lord, I was too busy, too focused to think about it. I had decided to forget a relationship. Then you shot into my room like a cannonball, and my life hasn't been the same." He laughed.

Kenann smiled as she remembered; then her expression sobered. "Danny Mac, what is going to happen to us?"

"What do you mean?"

"What happens next?"

"Well, I plan on taking you back to bed and getting all willy-nilly."

"I'm serious. What have you and Carter decided we are doing about the society?"

"I thought we were not going to think or talk about that while we were here. We have a plan. It will be okay."

They brought their plates over to the table and sat down. They devoured their meals. Apparently, they both had worked up an appetite.

"It's funny, I haven't had a single dream since we figured out I was being targeted. It's like that tactic was discovered so they abandoned it," she mused.

"Yes, and they also don't have access to trigger your hypnosis. I am sure that drove a lot of your dreams. It will be our job to figure out what their next plan is. But for now, what do you say I bring our mattress out here and we sleep by the fire?"

"I'd say, bring on the heat."

He made a grab for her. She dodged and ran giggling into the bedroom.

16

KENANN WAS AWAKENED by Danny Mac in the most delicious way. They had spent the last two days making love, talking, laughing, and cooking together in pure bliss. The dawn was breaking pink through the window. She raised her arms over her head and stretched languidly as Danny performed his magic.

"If I had known all this, I wouldn't have postponed this marriage thing."

"Satisfied?" he asked.

"What do you think?" She felt his smile against her skin.

A few minutes later, Danny had finished making coffee as Kenann came out of the bathroom. They smiled at each other.

"Are we pathetic?" she asked.

"A little, but who cares. Reality will hit soon enough. Here, take your coffee out on the porch. I'll be out in a minute."

The watcher zeroed in on the front door. He verified that it was the woman. Despite the efforts to make the hotel room at the Peabody appear to be occupied by two people, their maid was able to identify that only the CIA agent was staying there. They had a suite, and he was exiting from the other door. It had taken the watcher four days to track them. Now that he had visual on the target, he would call it in and await orders.

Kenann sat in one of the wicker chairs and drew her feet up under her. She smiled up at Danny Mac when he came out with his coffee and sat in the chair next to her. She loved just looking at him and being near him.

Danny looked over at her and saw her grinning. "What's up, James?" He laughed. "I mean, MacKenzie."

"Oh, just happy. Very, very happy."

"That's my plan. Are you relaxed?"

"Mmm" she purred.

Danny Mac laughed. He was delighted and a little surprised at the way Kenann had taken to their lovemaking. Once the initial shyness was gone, she was eager and willing. They were as suited in bed as they were in life, anticipating each other's moods and wants. These thoughts brought out his hunger for her, and it was evident on his face as he watched her. Kenann would never grow tired of seeing that look on his face. She sat down her coffee and got up. She moved to stand in front of him. Danny Mac looked up at her watching her intently. She slowly straddled him in the chair. He covered her hips with his hands. She put her fingers into his hair, cupping his face in her hands. She slowly took his mouth with hers. Her kisses were slow and languid, drawing him out and into her with skill he could not believe she possessed. No lover before her had been able to do this to him. He had a fleeting thought of the men who might be watching and knew he was the envy of all of them.

When he could no longer stand the branding of her body into his, he cupped her bottom in a secure grip and stood up, carrying her into the cabin. He did not bother to close the door. The fire inside was burning him alive. Kenann was biting his shoulder in her own sense of urgency. Danny Mac was reminded of the mating of the horses back on the ranch in Oklahoma. He could relate to the stallions right now with the intensity of his passion. He fell back on the bed wanting to shield her from his weight; but she rolled him over on top of her with surprising strength and speed. They hurriedly dispatched any offending garments and satiated themselves with a furious energy.

Danny Mac and Kenann had worn themselves out that day. It was if they could not get enough of each other; or maybe a premonition that their idyllic time was soon to be over. Danny Mac had made coffee the next morning when Kenann came in from the bedroom. They smiled at each other, remembering their recent passion.

"Good morning, beautiful. You look rested."

"Well, limbered up, to say the least."

Danny Mac laughed heartily. "Here's your coffee. I'll meet you on the porch."

Kenann wrapped an afghan around her shoulders to ward against the chill and opened the door. Her scream filled the morning air. She dropped her cup and knelt to tend to the person lying crumpled at her feet. Danny Mac was right on her heels.

"Get back inside!" Danny Mac barked.

"Oh, for goodness' sake! Let's get him in the house."

They worked together to gently turn him over. His head fell back and she saw it was Whittaker. He had been badly beaten. Danny lifted him into his arms as if he were nothing and carried him into the cabin.

"Bolt the door!"

She did then pulled accent pillows off the couch so Danny could lay him there. Kenann searched for a pulse. She felt a faint beat and nodded her head at Danny Mac. He pulled a handgun from the end table drawer and handed it to Kenann butt first.

He then pulled an assault rifle from under the couch and moved throughout the room, checking out windows and locking exterior doors as he called a number on his cell phone and spoke without preamble.

"They got to Whittaker. Report in." He listened as the person on the other end spoke. He came back to Kenann's side.

Whittaker moaned, and Kenann laid a comforting hand on his arm. She leaned in to hear what he was trying to say. She strained to make it out, and then it registered. "Infiltrated! Danny Mac, he is saying the men have been infiltrated."

Danny understood immediately. "Johnson, listen to me. One or more of your men is either dirty or has been overpowered. Yes, we are okay in here. Tighten your perimeter. Get eyes on everyone, and take this guy down."

Danny Mac took the pistol from Kenann and handed her his assault rifle. He raised an eyebrow in question. She nodded and began another sweep of their surroundings via the windows. Danny Mac got busy assessing Whittaker's injuries. He prodded and felt for broken bones. *None. That's good.* He palpated his abdomen as he had been shown by the navy corpsman who trained him on combat aid. He could not detect any overt abdominal or internal issues.

He leaned in close to Whittaker's ear, "John, can you hear me?" Whittaker emitted a grunt in affirmation. "Did you see who did this?"

Danny Mac leaned in closer to hear. "From behind. Saw his radio before I passed out. Our insignia."

"Okay, rest up, John. We will take care of it from here." He covered him with a blanket in the event of shock. His pulse was steady now. He had no way of monitoring blood pressure; but his respirations were even and unlabored. He surmised the beating had once again been meant to be a message: *You cannot hide from us. We are everywhere.*

Danny Mac joined Kenann who was standing to the side of the window, making sure she was not making herself a target. Danny Mac was impressed by her instincts. She was calm and focused. He took the time to thank God again for giving him this woman who was so perfectly suited to him.

"How is Whittaker?" She realized she had never known his first name. Of course Danny Mac did. He paid attention to detail.

"He will be fine, I think. Whoever did this only wanted to send another one of their messages. They are playing with us, and it is starting to really tick me off."

She reached up and touched his cheek. "Pardon the pun, but looks like the honeymoon's over."

He turned his face to kiss her palm. "Never."

17

JOHNSON STOOD STONE-FACED by Whittaker's bed. Mrs. Gage sat on the other side, holding Whittaker's hand. "Are you sure you don't want me to call your mother?"

"No, Ma'am. I mean, yes, Ma'am. I don't want you to call my mom. She thinks I have a desk job. You'll just scare her."

"Young man, that is very sneaky of you. If you were my son, I would whip your butt."

Despite the pain in his jaw, he cracked a smile. "I bet you would."

At that moment, Kenann, Danny Mac, and Carter walked into the bedroom. They had moved all operations back to Mrs. Gage fortress of a home. Johnson "came to attention" habit.

Carter motioned for him to stand down. "John, are you up to a briefing?"

"Yes, sir."

"Luckily, all the rooms in this gothic nightmare are big enough for a crowd. I will bring in everyone, and we can get started"

Jake pulled chairs into a semicircle around the bed. Rough, who had resided with Mrs. Gage during the short-lived honeymoon, sat in front of Kenann, leaning back on her leg. Granny James and Judy had their heads together, discussing something. Angelo, aka David, sat quietly beside Danny Mac, the only person with whom he truly felt comfortable. He could not believe that these people had welcomed him into their circle after what he had done to them.

Carter marveled at his hesitation to take the floor. He found himself looking to Mrs. Gage who gave him a slight nod. *Who was this woman who could exhibit such subtle command?* He wasted no time. "Folks, my original intent was to have you *assist* me in our investigation. Now I am resolved that you will be my only investigative team. At this point, I can trust no one else. Not even the president. Who knows how far or deep this operation goes. I will have to file reports to keep them off my back, but I am letting you know where it stands. We are it. Binegar was taken out swiftly. He never saw it coming. How they tracked us to the cabin and infiltrated our surveillance is beyond me."

Mrs. Gage touched the small earpiece in her left ear. "Excuse me, ladies and gentlemen. It appears we have a security breach." With that, she left the room, followed closely by Danny Mac and Kenann.

Carter looked at Andy, raising both hands in disbelief. He shook his head and turned, following her out and motioned Johnson to come with him.

"I tried to prepare him for Mrs. Gage." Andy and Jake were laughing as they ran after the others. Whittaker tried to get up but Judy put a restraining hand on his shoulder.

"Hang on, tiger. We will sit this one out, okay?" He gave her a dirty look and leaned back on his pillows. Granny moved up to his bedside and patted his arm. Then he gave her a sheepish smile.

Angelo sat stone-still. Granny James looked at him and winked. He gave her a tentative smile in return. A few minutes later, they were back. Blade was tucked under Jake's powerful arm. He sat him down in the middle of the group.

"What were you doing trying to sneak into this house? All you had to do was walk up and ring the doorbell."

Blade finally raised his head. "I didn't figure you would let me sit in on your meeting, and I was going to find a way to listen in."

"Why?"

"Andy said I was part of the team, and I want to know stuff." Jake looked up at Carter's impassive face. The silence was torture for Blade.

There was an unspoken agreement that this was Carter's call. He contemplated Blade's performance during the often harrowing events of the past summer as related by the team. He also had him investigated in the weeks following their return and knew that he had not revealed one iota of his experience, not even to his mother. He decided. "Okay, you're in, kid."

There was a combined whoop of emotion from the crew. Even Rough barked his approval. Blade beamed.

Mrs. Gage interrupted the revelry. "Blade, does your mother know where you are?"

"Ummm…no, Ma'am."

"Then I suggest you call her and tell her."

"Could you do it, Mrs. Gage? She always worries that I show up uninvited."

"Imagine that."

Everyone laughed.

18

THEY SETTLED BACK into the meeting in earnest with the addition of Blade setting on the floor between Andy and Judy's feet, who grinned at each other over his head.

Once again, Carter had the floor and wasted no time laying it out. "Since these guys had such an effective fail-safe escape plan, they left nothing to review. Our guys ran an analysis as to the people reported missing all over the world. Katarina was right, Danny Mac. They came from all walks of life. From hotel housekeeping staff to heads of state. All of them now have new identities, new lives somewhere."

Danny Mac spoke, "So have we looked back for clues?"

"What do you mean?"

"Katarina told me that this society had its beginning in the earliest civilization of ancient Sumeria."

"Which is now Iraq."

"Yes. Is there anything from ancient texts that might give us some clues?"

"Well, seeing as how they left no footprint in this century, it is unlikely. That is how they have remained under the radar all these years—millennia, really. But you brought up a good idea. It won't hurt us to do some snooping around through history."

Mrs. Gage queried, "Six thousand years of it?"

Judy laughed. "Have fun, guys. I have to go to work tomorrow."

They all turned and looked at her. Carter shook his head. "I'm afraid that won't be possible. I meant what I said. You are now my team, and that means all of you, full-time. I'm sorry, young lady."

Andy felt her stiffen beside him and quickly interjected, "We can work out the details later. Let's discuss our game plan now."

Judy raised an eyebrow at him but remained silent. She had agreed to help in any way she could; but she also had a job to do.

Carter continued, completely unaware what he had escaped from Judy. "We determined that one course of action was to try and flush this bunch out by using ourselves as bait. We get them to show themselves by coming after us. Then we move on to our next location and keep them on the defensive. We leave a small team behind to take note of any abnormality before joining us at our next destination. By doing this, we may be able to develop a profile of how they operate."

Blade spoke up, "I can help."

Danny Mac sighed. "Blaaade."

"No, really, I can. I did it before. You know I did."

Jake jumped in. "Yes, you did, but that was because you were a stowaway and before we knew what we were up against."

Danny Mac added, "Blade, you were a big reason we were successful. You found the command center and we were able to download information. You were a pro on that platform and getting us out of the cavern. And that is the truth, you know it. But there is no way we are going to take you with us. You are ten years old, and we love you. Not happening."

Blade pouted.

Carter continued, "Obviously, we will have to rely on others besides ourselves for logistics, but my goal is to keep any key element of our plans to ourselves. Things we want our adversary to know, we will put it out there. Otherwise, we are on information blackout. Understood?" There was general consent in the room. "Now as to some of the particulars, Judy, you and Kenann will be added to our payroll as will Danny. Mrs. Gage, I assume you will disdain our government's money. Mrs. James and Jake, what do you say?"

They sat in stunned silence for a length of time. The comrades in arms looked from one to another. They had come together because of their bond, not as a job. This felt off somehow. The mechanics of getting a government paycheck was a natural progression of what Carter was proposing; but it hit all of them in uncomfortable spots.

Danny Mac turned to Carter. "Can you give us a few?"

Carter looked confused and a little put out but complied. Johnson stayed at Whittaker's side in unspoken allegiance. Their involvement with this group in Egypt cemented their relationship.

Judy was the first to speak. "Danny, I don't like this. I *have* a job. This is who I am. I am a nurse."

Kenann added, "I am supposed to be on medical leave from my job."

Mrs. Gage weighed in. "It is one thing to offer our services, but entirely another to be taking orders from Mr. Carter." Johnson snickered. Everyone looked to him and grinned. It broke the tension.

Jake offered, "Folks, we knew it was coming to this. What do we want? Not to do this?"

Judy said, "Well…no."

Granny James spoke finally, "We have become a little family, haven't we? And to be paid to do what we feel like we have to do rankles a bit, I know. But if we allow Carter to pay those who need it…well, it can't be helped. It will just allow us to do what we are going to do anyway. It doesn't need to change a thing, my loves."

The air in their lungs deflated. They looked at each other. An agreement was reached. Andy went in search of Carter.

Judy looked at Mrs. Gage with a determined eye. "I'm only taking orders from you."

Mrs. Gage smiled. "I appreciate that, dear, but I am not sure that will always be practical. We will endeavor to play nice until such time that we…won't."

They both laughed in shared conspiracy.

19

CARTER CONTINUED THE briefing. "Andy, you and Judy will stay behind for a week or longer, if needed, to do surveillance on any unusual activity that occurs in Memphis after we leave."

Mrs. Gage interjected, "I will make sure any information my sources uncover will also be available to you as well."

Carter turned his eyes to Mrs. Gage but gave up any thought of questioning or challenging her. He knew it would be futile. He continued, "The rest of us will travel first to Istanbul where, literally, East meets West. I do not have time to send in an advance team this time. But when we move on to London, I will have Danny and Kenann go on first to develop a baseline of the status there. Once the rest of us arrive, we can assess any changes in activity or chatter."

Angelo finally spoke, "If they are watching you—and you know they are—won't they be tipped off by Danny and Hafsa's arrival?" He did not realize he had used his nickname for her. Kenann smiled. She secretly loved her *little lion* moniker.

"We will be using private transport, thanks to Mrs. Gage. We can only hope to slow down their tracking of our whereabouts." Angelo nodded his head in understanding. "And in this fashion, we are going to play hopscotch across the globe until we can build some sort of profile, flush them out, or force them into a showdown."

Blade had obtained permission to spend the night and would be rooming with Jake again. He was elated. Danny Mac and Kenann held hands as they went up the wide marble stairs to their room. Rough had looked at them reproachfully as they left him in the kind care of Granny. When they rounded the corner of the long hall, beyond the sight of those below, Danny Mac pushed Kenann back against the wall and plundered her mouth. Kenann was breathless when he tugged her hand to lead her down to their rooms.

"I've been wanting to do that in this house for a long time."

"I had no idea." Kenann laid her hand on her chest to calm her beating heart.

"Oh, you did too."

"No, really, I didn't. I couldn't understand why you wanted to marry me, Danny. I had no idea you felt *this* passionately about me."

"Well, if the last week hasn't proven it to you, I can see I have my work cut out for me. Before, I had to really watch myself. The man I used to be would have had you in a heartbeat. But the man I am and want to be had to keep our *marriage bed pure*."

"Huh?"

"Oh, it is a phrase used in the book of Hebrews."

"Well, all I can say is, I'm glad we are married now and I'm glad we waited—*you* waited—because I would have given in if you'd have asked me."

"I know that. It was up to me to make this happen."

"It is special, Danny Mac. Thank you."

"You are very welcome. Now let's make up for lost time." He whisked her into the room. She giggled as he kicked the door behind them.

"They look so happy." Granny scratched Rough's head as she and Mrs. Gage enjoyed a glass of wine together.

"Yes, they do. It makes me very happy for them."

"Sounds like we are off on another adventure. Do you think we are up to it?"

"Of course we are, Moira. We have to be. There is too much at stake. These kids and much more."

"Mr. Carter did not ask you, but can you trust all the people who work for you? You seem to have limitless resources and contacts."

"Well, I would love to say with full assurance that all my people are trustworthy. I truly think they are, but as precaution, not one person knows enough to hurt me. I have made sure of this for a long time."

"Is that why you are so secretive with us?"

"Oh, Moira, you don't know how much I want to share my life with you—with all of you. But I cannot. And this situation is a perfect example of why I can't. There are too many lives at stake that are depending on me."

"You have said that before. That is a pretty heavy burden you have chosen to carry."

"Sometimes I think it has chosen me. It's all I've known for so many years. I hardly remember anything else."

"Is it possible we could help you when this is resolved?" Mrs. Gage threw back her head and laughed. Rough raised his head and thumped his tail at the sound. The sudden image of involving this crazy crew in her passion was overwhelming. Granny James persisted. "Gabrielle, I am being sincere."

"I know you are, love. It's just that I have been on my own so long, and the thought of involving anyone in my efforts is impossible. But if I were ever to consider anyone for intimate inclusion in my work, it would be you and our wonderful entourage."

"Well, keep us in mind. We have proven quite handy in these things." Granny James raised her glass. Mrs. Gage joined her in the toast.

Angelo sat quietly with Blade and Jake. They teased each other over a board game they were playing.

"Want to play?" Blade looked up and asked him.

"Oh, no. I will sit and watch. But thank you."

Jake joined in the conversation. "Angelo, are you okay being here with us?"

"I was very happy to be asked to come here. But being here is a little uncomfortable, I have to admit."

"I have to ask, have you been contacted by the society?"

"No, I covered my tracks very well with the help of Andy and Danny." He looked uncomfortable and added, "Do not tell Carter they helped me."

Jake laughed. "It's alright, son. He figured they did. Don't worry about it."

"I have told Carter everything I can remember about the operation. Katarina didn't allow us to know much. We really were glorified errand boys."

"Will you go back to Amsterdam?"

"No, I quit my job and closed up my apartment."

"I'm sorry this thing is disrupting so many lives."

"It is fine. I will do anything Danny asks me to do."

"You know he doesn't expect anything from you."

"All the more reason for me to be loyal to my friend."

"Well, welcome to our team."

Blade raised his palm, and Angelo gave him a high five as he smiled.

Judy and Andy sat curled on the couch in the downstairs parlor before heading upstairs for the night.

Carter came through looking for a book to read. "I need you to stay focused, O'Hanlon."

"He is focused, *sir*. Don't you worry about Andy and me. We will get the job done. And what we do otherwise is absolutely none of your business."

"When you work for me, young lady, everything is my business."

"Then you'd better wrap your mind around me and Andy being together. Period."

"Are you threatening me?"

"However you want to look at it."

"Well, in that case, carry on." Carter caught Andy's eye on his way out the door and winked.

Judy hissed, "*Oooh!* That man irritates the fire out of me." She looked at Andy, "What's so funny."

"You, tiger. Now give me a kiss. I love you."

20

THE NEXT MORNING Jake, Carter, Andy, Angelo, and Danny Mac sat behind closed doors, developing their surveillance plans. Mrs. Gage drove Blade home to get ready for school and then took him there followed by their security detail. Blade loved riding in Mrs. Gage's sports car.

Judy went to work, despite Carter's objections, and put in her notice. She refused to just walk away. She told her supervisor she had a situation come up that was going to require that she leave town. She apologized for the short notice (she could only give them a week); but they were understanding and assured her they would give her a good reference. She then called her parents and told them she had taken an exciting new job that would allow her to travel. They didn't care what she did now that she was happy again. They had never learned of the sexual assault she had endured during that summer mission trip. They only knew she changed for several years; but now they had her back. That is all that would ever matter to them. The office rumor mill ran fast through the medical complex. Interested parties, who wondered where she was going, wasted no time sending the information to their control.

Kenann went to her office as well—an office she had spent no more than a few weeks in since she was hired. She met with Mr. Kesselring who hired and mentored her during her short tenure. She gave him her resignation letter, and he motioned for her to take a seat.

"Kenann, are you okay?"

"Yes, I am, Mr. Kesselring. I feel badly that I have not given a better performance for you. You have been very kind."

"Well, first of all, you never needed to perform for me, Kenann. I wish you could have been a part of our office. I think you would have been a great asset."

"Circumstances have dictated my life recently. I do not want to keep you hanging so I am going to resign my position so you can get someone in to do the job. I am going to miss my little office, though." She smiled at him.

"Kenann, don't give up on us. You have a place here anytime you want it."

"I appreciate that, Mr. Kesselring. I really do."

"I am not sure what your situation is but I wish you the best. Are you sure you're fine?"

"Yes. Did you know I recently got married?"

"No." He smiled at her. "Congratulations!"

"So you see, I am fine. Happy. And if my situation changes, I will give you a call."

"Please do that."

Before leaving the office, Kenann visited the office's public restroom. She no longer felt comfortable using the staff's. She came out of the stall and began washing her hands. When she glanced up at the mirror, she gasped in terror. Standing behind her was Pierre in a monk's hood. She stood frozen in place, unable to move. She forced herself to turn around in time to see the exit door closing. She ran out from behind the privacy wall of the restroom.

Chest heaving, she stood looking at the people sitting in the waiting area. Suddenly, they all looked suspicious. Her palms began to sweat. There was no sign of Pierre; but who could say that one of his people were not now watching out of the corner of their eye or perhaps ready to grab her. She sat down in the nearest chair and called Danny.

"What's up, kid?"

"Danny Mac—" her voiced cracked slightly. She willed herself to buck up.

"What's wrong? Where are you? Where is the man assigned to you?" Danny Mac was frantic.

"I'm okay, Danny. I'm sitting in a public place near people I trust. My man is waiting on me out front. But I want you to come get me. I saw Pierre. He was in a monk's hood."

"Are you sure?"

"Do you think I am seeing things?" Her voice was sharp. Unbeknownst to her, the listening man rejoiced at the distress in her voice.

"No, baby, I'm just rattled. Where are you? I'm on my way."

She gave him the necessary information and continued watching the people around her. Who was being called for appointments and who was lingering too long? They could be waiting on a family member and were not clients at all. The person in the monk's habit could very well have left the building as soon as they pulled off the disguise behind the privacy wall. *It wasn't Pierre. Too tall. It had been a cleverly crafted mask. Danny Mac was right!. They were mocking them. Showing off their reach and power.*

Danny Mac flew into the room and knelt down in front of her. She smiled at him. "I'm fine. It just shook me up a little. It will take more than a goon in a mask to get me."

The maniacal howl on the other side of the world unnerved those standing by.

21

KENANN PACED BACK and forth in front of Mrs. Gage and Mrs. James as they sat on the couch in the parlor. Judy had not yet returned from work.

"Now they are just starting to tick me off." The other ladies exchanged smiles when she began smacking her fist into her palm. "If they think some bozo in a mask is going to make me run scared, they have another thing coming." She stopped and pointed her finger at no one in particular. "I will kick their butts and hand them their heads." She turned and looked at the ladies. "What?"

Mrs. Gage spoke, "I appreciate your energy, dear. And you're cute."

Kenann straightened her shoulders. "I don't feel cute. I feel mean and ready to roll." The other women burst out laughing. Kenann turned to glare at them then succumbed to their humor. "Oh, you guys!"

Judy scurried into the room. "Andy just gave me the scoop. Whoa, this is *jacked up*!"

Kenann spread her arms palms up and nodded with emphasis. "I *know*!"

Judy flopped on the couch beside Granny James. "Mrs. Gage, what's the plan? The guys have been cooped up all day in that room upstairs. I can't believe you don't have it bugged or something." Mrs. Gage's enigmatic smile made them all pause.

Granny James laughed, "Gabrielle, tell me you're not doing that!"

"My dears, I am far too busy to sit in on boring meetings. I have a program that analyzes key words and provides me a summary report of salient facts after each of their sessions. And if you give me away, I shall claim complete deniability."

The female laughter charmed the men who were coming down the main stairway. They entered the room on a scene of tranquility, having no notion of the energy and subterfuge among their ranks.

Carter asked Judy, "When is your last day of employment?"

"This Friday. I don't like it, but they were really good about it so it made it easier."

Kenann asked, "What are our arrangements?"

Carter raised his hand and said, "We will take care of the details. Don't worry about them."

Kenann gave him a cheeky smile, belying her intent. "You forgot to call me, honey."

"Excuse me?"

"Did you or did you not offer me a job?"

"I did."

"And I'm sure you have some sense of the strength of the women in this room."

"I have never doubted that."

"Well then, I suggest you stop shutting us out of the information loop. I get that we don't need to know every detail, but you had better wake up to what is going on around you. We are a very tight group. If you want to be a part of our team, you'd better plan on bringing all of us to the table."

Carter did not respond immediately. Kenann did not flinch or waver. She was fired up, itching for a good fight. "Point taken. We will endeavor to do just that."

"Good. Don't forget it."

Carter gave her a look that said, *Don't push it.* Kenann returned one that said, *Bite me.*

Andy leaned in and whispered to Danny Mac, "I'm starting to feel a little sorry for Carter."

Danny Mac knew better than to laugh.

"Are you okay?" Danny Mac rubbed Kenann's back as she lay in his arms.

"Yeah, why?"

"Well, you looked ready to rip Carter's head off tonight."

"Or other body parts."

"Are you sure you aren't part sailor?"

"Well, you must remember I have been in almost every port in the world. I tend to be a little salty."

"And by the way, how did you learn to handle an assault rifle the way you did back at the cabin?"

"Remember my dad's pilot? The one who taught me martial arts? He was great. He spent more time and took more of an interest in me than either of my parents. He taught me how to ride, shoot, fight, and spit like a man." She laughed.

"Remind me to thank him someday."

Kenann sobered. "He was flying the plane that went down with my parents."

"I'm sorry, Kenann."

"Yeah, sometimes I feel guilty because I miss him more than I do Mom and Dad."

"But about tonight, are you okay?"

"Yeah, I guess. I am mad. I hate being played. And this stupid group is playing us and that just...*oooh*," she growled. "It really ticks me off."

"And Carter?"

"Oh, he is insufferable, but I guess I vented my spleen on him."

"It did my heart good."

22

THE ENTIRE GROUP including Blade came together on Friday night. Andy and Judy had been given their instructions earlier. They would be checking flight manifests for names of anyone who may be following them to Istanbul and who to watch for in the future. They decided to fly commercially on this first leg to draw their enemy out. Carter had pulled some strings to get a running list of any missing persons who were reported in the next week or so. Andy had an enormous database at his disposal to use for cross-reference. This would give them an idea of anyone who simply walked away from their lives to follow the team. They knew it was a long shot; but they were willing to try anything to get a bead on this group.

Mrs. Gage had heard from CJ Baer that he was scheduled to pick up some people in Baltimore and smuggle them into Canada. Mrs. Gage made sure he had numbers for her team of lawyers in case he was caught. She informed Carter of this plan that evening. He simply stared at her. She had a fleeting curiosity regarding what he might be thinking and a wiser mind prevailed. She did not ask.

Blade was given an assignment too. He was to watch Mrs. Gage's estate and Danny Mac and Kenann's place for any suspicious activity and to contact Carter directly if he spotted anything. He was beyond thrilled with this responsibility and was obviously going to take it very seriously. Carter would continue Blade's security detail as a precaution.

During the evening, Kenann found time to pull Judy aside. "How you doing, Jude?"

"Good. I'm good."

"How are you and the G-Man doing?"

Judy smiled. "Excellent."

Kenann returned her smile. "This romance thing is pretty sweet, huh? Are you going to marry him?"

"Oh, Kenann! I can't think about that. Not right now."

"Why not, for pity's sake?"

"Too much to think about."

"Bull-malarkey!"

"Excuse me?"

"You heard me. Believe me, if there is one thing I know, it's being scared. And you are scared."

"So what if I am."

"Listen, I was, too, for very different reasons. But don't let that stop you from having a wonderful thing."

"What if I am too screwed up to be a proper wife to him?"

Kenann stopped in the middle of firing back an answer. She knew this was a very real concern for Judy. She prayed quickly and decided. "So sleep with him and see."

"What?"

"You heard me. You love him, right? Is he is *the one*?"

"Well, yes, but—"

"No buts. If that is the only thing keeping you apart, find it out. If you can't go through with it, then you can maybe get therapy or something, but if you can move on from the trauma of your past, then there is no reason *not* to marry Andy."

"Do you really think I should?"

"Well, I can't guarantee it is the right thing to do, but it makes sense to me. I mean, you guys are kind of married in your hearts now. You can have the legal ceremony later. But to be on the safe side, don't tell Andy or Danny Mac this was my idea, okay?"

Mrs. Gage made arrangements for them to be taken to the airport by a limousine van service that Saturday morning. Goodbyes were said in the parking area in front of the mansion. Judy and Andy were to be staying on their surveillance detail before joining the others. The house and the grounds had a top-of-the-line security system and the manpower that Carter was using. Their current detail had been scrutinized further; but Carter told Andy to take no undue chances with them in the event any of them were dirty. Judy now had her own concealable handgun and a quick course in how to use it.

Blade was there to see the group off as well. He looked sad. Danny Mac sat beside him on the front steps.

"Hey, buddy, it will be okay. You have to take care of stuff here."

"Yeah, big deal."

"It is a big deal, dude. You have been in on everything from the beginning. You know what to look for. We are counting on you for intel while we are away. You have Carter's private number, right?"

"Yeah."

"Did you know that the president and a very few other people in the world are the only ones who have that."

"He made me memorize it and promise to never to write it down."

"See? You are a big deal." Blade beamed. Danny Mac continued, "I checked with your mom first to make sure it was okay. You will be in charge of working with Rough while we are gone."

Rough took that moment to stand by Blade and thump him with his tail in approval. Blade draped his arm across Rough's shoulder. He squared his shoulders and said, "I won't let you down, Danny Mac."

"I know, kid."

Granny James took Judy's face in her hands. "Follow your heart."

Judy's eyes widened. "Wait, what? Have you talked to Kenann?"

"No, why?"

"Well, what do you mean?"

"I just mean that even though we have to save the world from bad guys doesn't mean we can't carve out a little bit of this world for our own happiness. For the life of me, I don't know what's wrong with you, young folks. When I met Kenann's grandfather, I went for it. None of this pussyfooting around."

Judy laughed. "You are right, Granny. I'm going for it."

"Now that's my girl. Knock his socks off."

"Granny!"

Granny chortled and patted her cheek again. "See you soon, love. I want a ring on that finger," and walked away.

Judy stood staring after her.

All goodbyes were said. Blade and Rough stood between Andy and Judy, waving until they were out of sight.

Andy rubbed his hands together and winked at Judy. "Well, let's get busy, shall we? I shall now show you two how to be international spies."

Blade beamed. "Cool."

The flight to Istanbul routed them through Frankfort for a layover. Everyone gathered their carry-on luggage for the trek to their connecting flight. All were alert to subtle nuances in the behavior of the passengers around them. Who was being overly friendly and inquisitive? Who was quiet but watchful?

Danny Mac leaned into Carter. "Dark-haired woman in red dress."

Carter did not look her way. "Got it."

Kenann surreptitiously took a photo of the woman with her smart phone on silent. Sure enough, she joined them in the waiting area of the flight to Istanbul. *One down, thousands more to go*, Kenann thought. She showed Carter the picture.

He told her to send it to his phone and then delete it. He would then transmit it to Andy via his secure line. Mrs. Gage had had her nose glued to her computer throughout the flight. She was back at it in the waiting lounge.

Danny Mac approached her. "What's up, Mrs. Gage?"

"Fascinating reading."

"Must be. You've barely surfaced."

"Remember when it was suggested that we might find some clues by looking back?" She refrained from referencing the society.

"Yes."

"Well, I have been doing some research online and have come up with some interesting things. I am going to assign each of you some research homework, and we shall have a council of war in Istanbul.

23

ANDY RECEIVED THE text about the woman from the plane and ran photo recognition on her, checking it against the flight manifest. She was a process analyst for a chemical plant and had originally boarded in Oklahoma. He did a further background check and found absolutely no red flags on her record. These people were good. He didn't question how Danny Mac picked her out or that she was truly part of the society. He had learned a long time ago not to bet against Danny Mac.

Blade and Rough had gone home. He said he would be back after school Monday evening if his mom let him. He would continue to ride his bike by Danny Mac's house on his way home from school to keep an eye on things. His security detail would be following Blade everywhere until their return. He could only hope they were solid but realized there was only so much of this he could control. He decided to take a page from Danny Mac's book and send a prayer up to the Big Guy to protect Blade. But he was *not* going to let anyone know he did that. They may recruit him for their "church club."

Judy was sitting at another computer, monitoring a surveillance program Andy had set up. She had been unusually quiet.

"Hey, how's it going, sweet cheeks?"

"Excuse me?"

"You heard me."

"Well, smarty-pants, it's going well." She softened it with a grin. "I hope I am doing this okay."

"Trust your gut. Look for something that doesn't fit or seems off. This stuff is more about intuition than you think. I have some more information coming in from DC that we need to go over. They ran a computer analysis on the demographics of the folks who disappeared and want me to look at it. We will go over it together. Two eyes are better than one. And besides, then I can cuddle with you on the couch." He grinned. He took notice that she did not feel the same way. "Hey, what's bothering you, Judy?"

"Nothing. Why?"

"Come on! I'm an analyst, remember? I am paid to notice things."

"It's just everything, you know? A lot to take in."

He got up and pulled her to her feet taking her in his arms. He simply held her for several seconds. "I keep forgetting you are new to my world. I am used to this. You will be too, soon enough. I was glad when they put us together on this assignment. I didn't relish being separated from you."

"Me either."

"Seriously?"

"Seriously."

"Judy, we haven't talked about things for a few days. You know I love you, right?"

"Yes."

"And…?"

She laughed. "And I love you, silly man."

"Okay, good. I guess I just need to hear it."

"Well, I do. And I do not say that lightly…or easily."

"I know that, baby."
"I still worry."
"About what?"
"About being with you."
"Oh, honey! That will work itself out."
"What if it doesn't?"
"It *will.*"
"You can't know that."
"We will work through anything that comes our way. Even that."
Judy was still not convinced.

CJ Baer was pushing the envelope as much as he dared driving down I-40 to Memphis. He had rigged his trailer with listening devices and recorded all the conversations from Baltimore to across the border into Canada. He needed to talk privately to Mrs. Gage, ASAP.

Jake motioned to the group to gather around. "We have a few hours before we board our flight. I'm going over to that empty corner over there and set up the Lord 's table if anyone wants to commune."

Granny James said, "Thank you, Jake. That is so thoughtful of you."

Danny Mac, Kenann, Jake, and Granny James headed over to the deserted area of the lounge. Angelo (everyone had given up calling him David) asked if he could come. Danny Mac threw his arm over his shoulder and said, 'Sure!'

Carter leaned into Mrs. Gage. "What is he talking about, the Lord's *table*?"

"Every first day of the week, Christians meet together to *break bread* and commune with their Lord. They have been doing it for two thousand years since Jesus was on the earth."

"Well, that's just creepy. I spend my life fighting cults, and these guys are right smack in the middle of one."

"I used to think so myself. But these last several months with Jake and Danny Mac have changed my mind a bit. It bears looking into, Mr. Carter."

"I'll say. I have been watching them for years."

"Have you found them to be subversive or dangerous?"

"I have found a fair number of nut jobs in the bunch."

"Do you know what they believe or stand for."

"Hey, I went to Catholic school. I'm not a complete idiot."

"They have something, Mr. Carter."

"Oh, great! If you join their cult, I'll be outnumbered and probably get murdered in my sleep."

"If you are murdered in your sleep, it won't be because of that, my friend."

He looked at her askew, and then they both burst out laughing,

24

JAKE BROUGHT OUT the leather box from his carry–on, which contained a small bottle of grape juice and unleavened bread. He set them out beside his Bible and read from 1 Corinthians 11:25-29 then commented, "We take this bread and drink this fruit of the vine every Lord's Day to remember Jesus's death on the cross for the sins of the whole world and his resurrection that gave us victory over death and ultimate victory over Satan. We have embarked on a mission to fight evil. We need the Lord's strength and guidance on this quest and we remember him over this table that is spread before us. Danny Mac, will you ask the blessing for the bread?"

Danny Mac bowed his head along with the others. "Lord, we love you and take this time to remember your sacrifice. We thank you for your love for us and your continued protection and care. Bless this bread from its common to its holy use. In Jesus's name, amen."

They passed the bread between them, taking off a small bite and placing it in their mouth. Angelo passed it without partaking. Jake then bowed his head and said, "Lord, we come before you again, thanking you for your love and this memorial feast you instituted for us to remember you. We thank you for your blood represented by this fruit of the vine and for the power your Son's blood to redeem our lives and continually cleansing us from all sin as we walk with you. We love you, Lord. Bless this cup. In Jesus's name, amen."

They drank from the small cups of grape juice. Jake asked them if anyone had anything on their heart. Kenann spoke up. "Can we meet together regularly for prayer?"

"Sure, honey," Jake replied.

Granny James added, "We mustn't neglect our other team members. We must make them feel comfortable to meet with us too. We don't want anyone to feel excluded."

Danny Mac smiled at his sweet in-law. "You are right, Granny." He paused. "Except Carter. Him, I could exclude." He grinned.

Granny James' tone was admonishing. "Daniel Joseph McKenzie."

As they were boarding their plane for Istanbul, Danny Mac came up behind Kenann and whispered softly so no one else could hear, "Want to join the *Mile High Club*?"

She glanced back and elbowed him in the gut. "I will not ask if you are already a member." He had the good sense not to reply.

They arrived in Istanbul late at night. The woman in the red dress had remained watchful throughout the flight as did the watched. She hurriedly checked through customs in order to contact control and get in position to further her surveillance. Carter made it through customs first so he kept vigilance to see if she passed off to another person; but she seemed to remain the primary tail at this point. He waited on the others to join him.

At Danny Mac's urging, Carter had deferred to Mrs. Gage about making logistical arrangements.

"She can do more in her sleep than we can begin to pull together in a lifetime," Danny Mac said.

Carter had not been disappointed. He was becoming more than a little impressed—and he dared admit, enamored—with the diminutive little dynamo. Jake had stolen Danny Mac from him. Maybe he would take the little beauty for himself and leave Jake in the dust. An interesting thought, but now it was time to move to the next phase.

CJ Baer rolled into town very early in the morning. He pulled his rig into the truck lot and slept for a while. Mrs. Gage always had a rental car available for him when he came into town. He waited until a decent hour and drove over to her house. A small boy was coming out of the door, followed by a tall man in a suit. CJ took note of the bulge of a gun under his jacket. They stopped in their tracks and both looked at him with a steely eye. He would have laughed at the way the boy mimicked the man if he didn't want to trigger the man's anger.

"Can we help you?"

"Is Mrs. Gage around?"

"Why do you need to know?"

CJ could feel his irritation rise. "Well, for one thing, she asked me to come here. Who are you?"

"A friend."

"So am I."

Blade suddenly remembered. "Wait, are you CJ?"

"Yes, young man, I am."

"Andy, this is the truck driver who was bringing us intel."

"Intel?" Andy and CJ exchanged a smile.

"I do have intel."

"Well, Blade, I am going to take you to school and then this gentleman and I will talk."

"Oh man! Why do I miss all the cool stuff."

"You are our undercover kid. You have the coolest job of all."

"Yeah, right. You are just saying that to shut me up." He accepted defeat. "Maybe I'll see you around, Mr. CJ."

"Count on it, kid." He smiled at him. Blade liked him and hoped he would get to see him again.

Andy nodded at CJ and put his arm around Blade to steer him to his car. He said over his shoulder, "Hang tight for a few. I'll be back." He called Judy and told her to leave the guy cooling outside until he got back. Then he called the security detail to also keep an eye on him in case he was not who he claimed to be.

CJ got back in his car. He took note that he was not invited to go in. That was fine. He was glad to see they were being cautious. With what he overheard, they need to be. He had listened to the people he was smuggling into Canada for several hours. They moved around freely until they got to the border; at which point, they went back into their shipping containers, and CJ sealed them in. He prayed the whole time they wouldn't be discovered. He knew Mrs. Gage would make it right; but he didn't want the hassle.

Andy was only gone a little while. He walked by the car and motioned CJ into the house. He followed him through the door and into the parlor to the right. He noticed a gorgeous blond sitting on the couch, who raised an inquisitive eye at the man.

"CJ, this is Judy. I'm Andrew. We work with Mrs. Gage. What have you learned?"

Well, so much for niceties. "Mrs. Gage asked me to take a certain load to Canada. It contained several people that needed to get out of the country so I installed a listening device. They were agitated and running scared and mad. They talked about what they wanted to do to the—pardon my language, Ma'am—bitch who did this to them. They were meeting in different places around the world to regroup. One man was on his way to Athens; another to Madrid. One of the ladies was going to London. They could not wait to see what the *master* would do to some person named *Inanna*."

"Master?" Andy jumped on that. "What else did they say about the *master*?"

"Let me think. They said he would not rest till the order was avenged."

Judy and Andy looked at each other. "Did they give any indication where the master is?"

"No, not really, but they all seem to be in contact with him. Pretty direct contact. It was like they all knew everything at once and were just discussing what they were hearing."

"They said this Inanna had ruined everything. They had good lives they had to leave behind. Now they had no idea what kind of life the order would ask them to live. They left their spouses and kids and jobs. Crazy! But, mainly, they were mad. I pity this Inanna if any of them get their hands on her."

"Where did you take them?"

"To a warehouse on the waterfront. I have the address I can give you. They paid me in cash and said to get lost. If I talked, I'd die."

"Do you think it was wise to come here? They know who we are."

"Doesn't matter. Mrs. G said I come here so I come here."

"Well, you may need to lay low for a while. Do you work for a company?"

"No, I own my own rig."

"Well, plan on staying here for the time being. Mrs. Gage would have my head if I got you hurt."

"I'm not worried about it. I can take care of myself. Besides, I have Freddie."

"Freddie?" Judy finally spoke.

CJ laughed. "Yeah, my cat."

Judy grinned. "Sounds like you're covered then."

Andy pressed, "Seriously, dude. Stay here, okay?"

"All right, for a few days. But Freddie has to stay too."

"That is no problem," Judy offered.

"Good. That's settled." Andy spoke to Judy. "I need to go up and contact Carter and Mrs. Gage with this." He got the address of the drop off from CJ. "I want to see what they want us to do next."

25

AFTER CJ TALKED directly to Mrs. G, he decided to pick up his things from his truck. She asked him to stay at her home until further notice. Judy asked him to wait on Andy. She knew he would want him to have backup. Andy came in and confirmed this. He contacted Mrs. Gage's butler who also acted as her security chief. He alerted them that Judy would be alone and to be vigilant.

His response was a very British, "Very good, sir."

Andy bent down and kissed Judy. "Stay put, beautiful. No wandering off."

"Yes, dear." Her tone was sarcastic but she softened it with a smile.

CJ inquired as they got in the car. "What has Mrs. G got herself into now?"

"It's a pretty big mess. How do you know Mrs. Gage?"

"She bailed my kid sister out of a jam. We made friends, then one thing lead to another. I'd die for that woman."

They drove in silence the rest of the way to the truck stop next to the interstate. He pulled in beside his rig. Andy reached a hand over to stop him as he started to open the car door. "Hang on."

They sat still for several seconds. CJ looked over at him expectantly, wondering what they were waiting on. Andy moved his hand palm down a couple of times as he opened his door. CJ understood. Low and slow. Andy pulled his service weapon. He motioned CJ to open the back doors of the box trailer, staying behind the door and keeping himself out of the way. Andy took out his flashlight and placed it above his pistol. He nodded at CJ.

When he reached and lifted the hasp on the door, all hell broke loose. The door slammed into his face and he flew backward, landing with his back on the pavement. Andy returned fire while diving out of the line of bullets flying from the back of the rig. Two men jumped down. CJ had already rolled under the trailer and grabbed his tire iron he had stashed there. He took out one of the guys out at the knees, who fired and missed CJ as he fell. CJ rolled out the other side of the trailer and met Andy behind a nearby vehicle.

CJ nodded at Andy's gun. "You got another one of those?" Andy grinned and pulled a .380 from his back waistband.

"Don't shoot yourself. I don't want to fill out the paperwork."

"I think I crushed that guy's kneecap. He crawled behind that truck."

"Yeah, I saw that. Good work. I've called it in so the cavalry is on the way." Andy saw CJ's eyes move sharply. Before CJ could speak, Andy turned and shot the man fleeing from behind the truck.

"Pretty nice shooting." CJ laughed. "Should I go check that other guy?"

"Better wait. He is still armed. Let's see if we can flush him out." He called out, "Hey, Mac! Want to give up?"

The response made them both raise their eyebrows.

CJ asked, "Is that even possible?"

Andy laughed. They heard the sirens. Andy told CJ to stay put and keep an eye on the injured man. He ran to the front of CJ's truck and motioned for the uniformed officer who arrived first. He was able to communicate to the officer that one man was down and another was still armed. He gave him his general location. As the Kevlar-clad officers moved in, a single gunshot sounded. He turned back and looked at CJ, who shook his head. They wouldn't be getting any information out of these men.

The crowd, which had hunkered down in place at the sound of gunfire, came out in droves when the police started putting up the crime scene tape. They gathered around the limits of the perimeter like moths to a flame. Andy had shown his badge and vouched for CJ. He explained they were mates, who had simply come back to the truck to get his things and interrupted a couple of guys trying to rob him.

Andy scanned the faces in the crowd, without appearing to observe. He began talking to one of the uniforms and kept his eye on an older man in his right peripheral vision. He looked practically homeless with a wizened beard and hooded jacket. But the eyes weren't right. He guessed he could be mentally ill; but there was venom directed straight at him. He ended his conversation and walked directly to the man. The old man's eyes never wavered.

Andy got in his face and growled, "Give a message to your boss, will you, pal?"'

The man didn't blink. "Tell him yourself." He flipped open his collar on his flannel shirt, revealing a mic. He flipped a switch for audio.

"Yes, Mr. O'Hanlon, you have a message?" The voice was mechanical and probably using a voice synthesizer.

Everything in Andy clenched, but he hissed. "We are coming for you—for all of you, you scumbag. You know that, don't you?"

"Oh, I'm counting on it. And I look forward to watching your little blonde beauty taken apart piece by piece."

Andy grabbed the man and snarled, "Anyone touches her, the hounds of hell won't stop me."

"Give Inanna my best regards. I have special plans for her too. So funny you should mention the hounds of hell. That is exactly who is coming for you," the mechanical voice made the words more sinister.

Andy knew it was pointless to try to take this guy in. He had nothing to charge him on. He removed his hands from the man's clothes with a satisfying little shove and walked away. He tagged CJ and nodded toward his car. "Got your stuff?"

"Yeah. Are we okay to leave?"

"Yep, they think we stopped them before they could take anything. They have your statement. We're good."

They got in the car and headed back to Mrs. Gage's home. When they came into the parlor and sat down, Judy raised an inquisitive eyebrow at Andy.

He said, "You know, I'm getting really sick of these people."

"Excuse me?" Judy said.

"They know our names. They know our relationship. They called you *my* blonde beauty."

"What? You *talked* to them?"

"Guy in the crowd had a comm device. Yep, just talked to one of the bastards myself."

CJ told Andy, "Dude, you're going to have to start from the beginning.

26

THEIR RIDE THROUGH Istanbul last night had given them majestic views of the Blue Mosque and Hagia Sophia. Istanbul was a beautiful city in which Europe and Asia were joined. Mrs. Gage had secured some nice digs once again.

Kenann did not care how she did it, she was just happy to stretch out on the luxurious bed, reveling in the view of the Bosphorus. She smiled when Danny Mac came in but sat up when she saw his face. "What is it?"

He sat down beside her and decided it was better to just get it over with. "Andy called. They had an encounter in Memphis." He hurried on as she stiffened. "Everyone is fine. He made contact with one of the members." Danny pulled her into his arms and held her. Despite her brave face, he knew she was remembering some very bad times and feelings.

"Have you been meeting with Carter?"

"Yes, me, Angelo, and Jake."

"Not Mrs. G.?"

Danny Mac laughed. "She was too busy to meet with us."

"What does she have up her sleeve now?"

"I don't know, but I think Carter is nervous. He kept asking where she was. You have to admit, Mrs. Gage on the loose is a dangerous proposition."

"Well, in the meantime, let's explore this villa for some food. I'm starving." She grabbed his hand, pulled him up, and wrapped her arm around his waist. She was so thankful to be facing this with him. Even the thought of going head-to-head with the society again was bearable as long as she had Danny Mac.

They were walking down the long corridor in their sock feet when they heard raised voices. Danny Mac recognized them immediately and put his finger to his lips. Kenann followed him as he tiptoed to the huge door leading into what looked like a library. The door was open a crack. They shamelessly listened to the heated discourse.

"You heard me, I said leave her alone."

"Oh, come on, Jake. What are you going to do about it?"

"She has been hurt enough in her lifetime. I won't stand by and watch her be hurt again."

"First of all, I don't intend to hurt her. My intent is to hurt you. And I repeat, what are you going to do about it?"

Jake chose to ignore Carter's goading. "I am asking you not to use her to satisfy this grudge you have against me."

"Too late."

"Carter, this is ludicrous. We have too much at stake to play a stupid game like this."

"Well, unlike you, I can handle more than one thing at a time. And a harmless flirtation will not impact my resolve to handle this situation. If I can rub salt into your wound while I'm at it… well, it's a win-win now, isn't it?" Carter laughed and slapped Jake on the arm before heading toward the hall.

Danny Mac picked Kenann up around the waist and ran down the hall to the first open door he came to. He slid inside just as Carter entered the hallway. Kenann started to laugh. Danny Mac covered her mouth with his. He was just getting into it when Carter walked by.

"Get a room." Danny Mac and Kenann fell against each other, trying not to laugh out loud.

"What in the world was that about?" Kenann whispered.

"More of Carter's stupidity."

"I assume they were talking about Mrs. G."

"Well, it better not have been you." He laughed.

"Should I tell her?" Kenann asked.

"No, it would only give it more credence. She is a big girl. She can handle herself."

"I feel sorry for Jake."

"I think he really cares for Mrs. Gage, but she is holding him at arm's length. Her choice, I guess. But Jake is right, we can't let this distract us. Now, come on. Let's go find that food. And then I need you to help me with my homework."

The next morning, they met in the large dining room. Mrs. Gage encouraged them to fill their plates at the sideboard and join her at the table. "I trust you all have completed your respective assignments?"

"As instructed." Carter smirked.

"I appreciate your cooperation. I needed the extra eyes to assist me on my theory. Daniel, what did you find?"

"The Coptic literature makes reference to what they call *infiltrations*—"

Mrs. Gage interrupted, "Did you detect any patterns that might be useful to us."

"I think so, but I'm not sure. I will be interested to hear the other results to compare and decide. There were some who declared that their belief system was being subtly manipulated.

It sounded very contemporary. These people were labeled the equivalent of conspiracy theorists." They laughed. "Of course, those were not the terms they used but it was the same. There was significant conflict in the literature between the two camps."

"But can we be sure it was the society?"

"No, but that's why I want to compare the other results. The efforts to subvert seemed pretty well orchestrated."

Mrs. Gage turned to the others. "David Angelo?" She had begun calling him by both names, recognizing it was a nice blend of the old and new persona and felt this fit him. He smiled at her. "What did you determine from the Russian information?"

"Just like Danny Mac, I was drawn to the ideological conflicts that emerged."

Kenann interjected, "But this has happened since the beginning of time. There will always be a difference of opinion on any subject."

Mrs. Gage said, "If we are to find any clues as to their modus operandi, we must look at these important junctures in history. By their own admission, they say they were there. Our job will be to find their footprint."

"*Madam President*?"

Mrs. Gage honed in on Carter, and despite herself, she laughed. "Mr. Carter, I realize you find it…chafing to work with me in this capacity, but I certainly defer to you."

"I am the top US analyst on this exercise. Want me to take the data and submit a report of similarities and patterns?"

She paused only briefly but he took note of it. "Yes. Everyone, please turn over your notes to Mr. Carter."

Jake sighed and shoved his papers on Nazi Germany across the table. Danny Mac, Angelo, and Mrs. Gage did the same with their respective folios on other high-profile points in the historical past.

Carter smiled and shuffled them into one pile. "I will have my report to you by the end of the day tomorrow."

"Thank you, Mr. Carter." Suddenly, she snapped alert. "We have a breach. Follow me and quickly."

She ran to one of the panels along the wall and pushed on the corner. It slid open silently. She stepped aside and ushered the others with haste. The door closed quietly behind them.

Kenann grabbed Mrs. Gage's arm and whispered, "Granny!" Her eyes were frantic. Mrs. Gage hesitated only a brief second. She looked at Danny Mac and nodded up the steps. She made a circle in the air and pointed down indicating all the rest of them were to go down. They complied without hesitation.

Mrs. Gage joined Danny Mac, and they ascended the steps to the next level. They could hear male voices and knew the sweep team had made it to the second floor. Neither spoke but both prayed they could get to Granny in time. Mrs. Gage found the panel to Granny's room and opening it a mere few inches. What they saw stunned them. Danny Mac stole a quick glance at Mrs. Gage and grinned. Granny had managed to pull a wooden slat from her bedstead and stood facing the door. She held the slat like a Louisville slugger ready to take on the world. Danny silently crept behind her, covering her mouth with his hand to silence any startled cry. She started to struggle but soon realized it was Danny Mac and allowed him to carry her through the panel into the passage. He sat her down.

Granny whispered, "I thought you'd never come."

Danny Mac grabbed her hand and pulled her into a crushing embrace. They silently made their way down the steps to the bottom level and walked into the large room where the other team waited. Kenann swallowed Granny in her arms, thanking Danny Mac with her eyes above Granny's head. Danny Mac thought once again how much he loved these two women.

Carter jumped first. "Do you mind telling me what the hell is going on?"

"I was notified that we had some intruders entering the house."

Kenann asked, "In broad daylight?"

"Apparently, the Turkish contingency of the society is not as subtle as others," Mrs. Gage replied. "The staff was all alerted to escape. They should all be here in a few minutes.

"How secure is this area?" Danny Mac asked.

"Follow me," she spoke as she walked. "There is a traditional basement above us to throw off suspicion of this much deeper bunker. There are visible exits to the outside from that level to promote the decision that we have left. Also, I am sure you noticed we came through another well-hidden and camouflaged door into this level, concealing it from the one above. We have separate water and air filtration systems in the event they try to flush us out with tear gas or the like."

The next room was stocked with food and firepower. She opened the next door to show several large SUVs.

"The entrances to this site are a few kilometers away and well-camouflaged. I think we are quite secure for the time being."

Carter was baffled. "How did you manage to construct this under the noses of the very restrictive Turkish government?"

Mrs. Gage responded, "Money has always been able to buy secrecy."

Just then, the house servants came into the kitchen/dining area and formed a line, looking at Mrs. Gage and awaiting orders.

"Wonderful job, ladies and gentlemen. Mr. Biggs, I assume you activated the locks on all the panels to prevent their discovery?" He nodded. "Now let's busy ourselves making accommodations for a short stay. Clean sheets and a bit of tea are in order."

The staff smiled at her and began busying themselves. Mrs. Gage turned to the rest of the group and gestured for them to sit at the awaiting long table.

27

"THEY ARE THE Jinn!"

"Nonsense."

"I tell you, they disappeared into thin air. There was no one in the house, and no one saw them leave."

"Then they are still there."

"We searched, I tell you. Their food was still warm on the tables. They have magical powers."

"Stay there. I'm coming."

"But sir—"

"I will be there in a few hours." His words and tone brokered no further objections.

From a villa high in the Alps, preparations were made for the master with his bodyguards and assassins to leave for Istanbul. He was not trusting anyone else to end this. He wanted to look into the eyes of Danny Mac and Kenann as he slowly and painfully took their lives. Yes, he decided he would make Danny Mac watch as he tortured and killed Kenann—or maybe the other way round. He still had plans for Kenann.

CJ appointed himself Blade's unofficial protector. The kid had really gotten to him. He had a great dad growing up and couldn't stand the thought of this kid not having one. It broke his heart. The security detail would remain in place; but CJ planned on being closer. Blade came to the mansion after school the next day.

Andy greeted him, "Hey, little dude. How ya doing?"

"I told my mom you were helping me with my homework."

Andy paled. "I've seen your homework. I can't do that fifth grade math."

Judy smacked Andy on the shoulder. "You're off the hook, big guy. I love math." Judy put her arm over Blade's shoulder, and they went to the library table next to the patio window.

"Whew! Dodged that bullet," he said to CJ. "Have you seen the way they do math now? It is ridiculous."

CJ laughed. "That's why I am driving a truck, man. Did Mrs. G tell you she wanted me to stay?"

"Yes, and I think it's a good idea. You will have added protection for yourself now that you are on the radar, and you can keep an eye out for Blade."

"One step ahead of you, brother. I'm going to need some firepower."

"She didn't say anything about that."

"Well, I'm saying it. I don't usually go around armed but after what happened at the truck yard, I will feel a whole lot better if I'm prepared."

"I hear you. I will get you hooked up. But don't go rogue."

CJ shot him a disgusted look. "Do I look like somebody who would do that? I didn't get this pot belly from fighting ninjas."

Andy burst out laughing. "Okay, I'll make sure you have anything you need before we take off."

"When will that be?"

"Soon. We have learned about as much as we can, I think. We have confirmed that the society has people strategically placed but can move them on a moment's notice. We have tracers and profiles out on anyone who has left their job or community suddenly. We have compiled extensive background and lifestyle data on them to track any patterns for recruitment or connections—that sort of thing. With facial recognition software, we have a better chance of tracking them and seeing where they are placed next. We can then put a watch on these people and, in turn, the society itself. Carter decided to farm out all that data to the techs at Langley to analyze. He wants the head of the beast. That is our job."

CJ asked, "Do you think the kid's safe?"

"I hope so. We have done everything we can to make sure of it but you never know, and that sucks."

"Well, I'm gonna do everything I can. Mrs. G is counting on me."

"And we are not about to disappoint her, are we?"

"Not on my watch."

Andy and Judy were sitting silently, curled up together on the couch. CJ had dismissed himself and gone up to bed after walking Blade home. They had spent the evening challenging each other on video games after Blade and Judy finished homework. Judy and Andy had smiled at each other, listening to them fight and laugh over the game. Now in the stillness of both the night and the house, Judy and Andy sat lost in their thoughts.

Andy broke the silence. "Marry me."

"What?"

"I love you, babe. Now I know how Danny felt. I can't do this without you. I need to be with you."

"But I've told you, I don't know if I can *be* with you, Andy."

"And I told you it will not be a problem."

"But you don't know that."

Andy gave her a devilish grin. "I have tremendous confidence on my ability to seduce you."

Judy could not help herself and laughed. Then she sobered. "I couldn't stand it if I disappointed you."

"Oh, babe! You could not do that. I have checked on it. We can fly to Vegas and make it legal. It will be too much of a hassle to do it here since I'm not a resident."

"You've put some thought into this."

"I take my job and this situation seriously, but to be honest, I think about you and being with you constantly."

Judy dropped her head. How could she make him understand how terrified she was of freezing up during their intimacy? She still had nightmares about the repeated rapes. What if she went total freakazoid on him during sex? That would not be fair to him. She was decided. "Can I give you my decision tomorrow?"

"As long as it is yes."

Judy took a deep breath and pushed the door open before she could change her mind.

Andy, wearing just his jeans, was standing at the window and looking out with a longneck bottle in his hand. He turned when he heard the door close. His eyes met hers. "Judy?"

"Before you say anything, I have thought about this and I know what I'm doing."

"And what *are* you doing?"

She took another deep breath. *In for a penny, in for a pound.* She dropped her robe. She wore the only thing she owned that wasn't flannel. By the way Andy's pupils flared, she guessed it worked.

"Judy—"

"Is that all you are going to say?"

"Yes."

"Well, this is very awkward."

"Judy, I have asked you to trust me."

"Oh, Andy! I do. It's me I don't trust."

"Are you that convinced we can't make it work in bed?"

"I don't know. I don't *know.* It's scary enough to get married but with this hanging over my head, it's like a brick wall. I can't get around or see around it."

"Come over her. Sit down." He motioned her to the two wingback chairs by the fireplace. She grabbed her robe from the floor and put it back on. *So much for the big sexy entrance.* She sat across from him and dropped her head. "Judy, I am honored—" she snorted in derision but he continued, "I said I'm honored that you would do this for me—for us. But it is not necessary."

"Maybe not for you, but it is for me."

"How so?"

"Look, the future is a big blank page to me. I know I may be a control freak but I have to know what I'm doing."

"Oh, for Pete's sake! You are making sex with me sound like a medical procedure you have to perform. What happened to passion and maybe a little lust thrown in?" His volume matched his annoyance.

"Well, I went for lust and you shut me down," she spat back but couldn't stop the tears from filling her eyes.

"Judy…" His tone was now soft and pleading.

"Forget it!" She jumped up and started for the door. Andy grabbed her arm before she could make it two feet. She froze. He loosened his grip and ran his hand down her arm. His relief was palpable when she allowed him to link his fingers with hers.

"Judy."

"What?" Her voice was defeated.

Andy turned her and pulled her into his arms. She went without resistance; her body limp in his embrace.

"Judy, I read this all wrong. I saw it as you making a sacrifice of your principles for me, and I couldn't let you do that, no matter how hot you look in that nightie." He bent down and looked at her with a grin. He saw a flicker pass her lips. "But I get it now. You have to do this. Not for me. For you."

Judy looked up and met his eyes. "Well, I may be the frigid one, but you sure know how to kill a mood." Judy grinned when Andy burst out laughing.

28

THEY FLANKED EACH other at one end of the long wooden table. Mrs. Gage sat at the head. Her house, her show. She leaned forward, tapping a pencil. "Well, according to the monitors, the rats have moved in upstairs, and it looks like they are making ready for the king rat to show up."

"That's good news, right?" Kenann looked from face to face for confirmation. "Why all the long faces?" She caught the looks they exchanged and also that Granny was looking down at her clasped hands on the table in front of her.

Danny Mac turned to Kenann. She turned too as the light began to dawn. "Kenann, one of our biggest goals was to keep this group off-balanced."

"This is where I come in." It was not a question.

"Yes, but only if you are comfortable."

"Hey, I didn't come all this way to sit it out when it starts getting interesting. We have already been through this. "

Danny Mac grinned; he knew she meant it. "That's my girl!"

"So what's the plan?" Again, Kenann looked to the others.

Carter had been quiet. He cleared his throat. "Well, since they thought it beneficial to mess with your mind, we thought we would return the favor."

"So what are you talking? Gaslight them?"

"Basically," was Mrs. Gage's reply. Granny had not looked up. Danny Mac took note of this too.

"Moira, are you okay?"

She looked up. "Yes, Danny. I'm just concerned about Kenann's safety. I am in agreement. I'm just…" she paused, "cautious."

"As are we, *Granny.*" Carter's voice dripped with sarcasm.

Jake leaned in menacingly. "Carter, it was you who asked all of us to come on board. So help me, don't you dare start giving us attitude now."

The two squared off visibly. Mrs. Gage looked between them with disgust building toward a good rage. When they didn't back down, she slapped her palms down on the table and stood.

"Enough!" she roared. "Carter, you chafe at my leadership, but you can't lead your way out of a wet paper bag. Nor do you know the *first* thing about managing people. And you, Jacob, are so concerned about everyone else, but you aren't man enough to go after what *you* want." No one was more shocked by her outburst than Mrs. Gage herself. She turned her back to the table to compose herself. She did not turn back; but said, "I am going to go to the control room. I would appreciate if no one followed me." She squared her shoulders and left the room.

After several seconds, Danny Mac broke the uncomfortable silence. "We are all cooped up here and getting edgy. We need to stay focused."

"You think?" Carter continued his sarcasm.

Before Jake could come across the table, Danny Mac said, "Cool it, Carter. Let's take a break. Everyone find a corner and get in it. We will regroup in a few."

Everyone stood and moved away from the table. Danny Mac took Kenann's hand and pulled her into one of the stone stairwells leading up to the main house. They sat side by side on the steps.

"What was all that?"

"Walls are starting to close in. Knowing that our mortal enemies are a couple stories up isn't helping."

"I get that. I was actually talking about Mrs. G. I felt sorry for her. Maybe we need to take a field trip."

Danny Mac glanced over in irritation. His patience was growing thin as well.

"Hey, don't give me a look. I'm serious. We are good at disguises. We have eyes on what is going on in the rooms upstairs, but maybe we can get some intel around town or what's happening around the house." Danny Mac was listening. "That, and we can quit feeling helpless. That will buy some good stress relief, Plus, we might learn something."

Danny Mac loved this woman. She was not just another pretty face.

Andy took Judy's hand and led her around the room, turning off lamps and leaving one burning low at the bedside.

She laughed as he pulled her along behind him. "What are you doing?"

"I am making sure you don't get away." When he had the lighting the way he wanted, he picked up his iPhone and found his music. Finding the file he wanted he put it down and turned to her. "I hope you don't think my music is too corny, but it works for me." He took her in his arms as Percy Sledge crooned "When a Man Loves a Woman."

"Dance with me, Judy."

She lifted her eyes to his and was overpowered with love. He was so patient. She reveled in the fact that she felt *no* fear with this man and what they were doing. This was love. This was right.

They swayed, enjoying looking at each other. The moment was pure joy. Andy ran his fingers up her arms and slipped her robe off her shoulders. He let it fall of its own volition while his hands moved up to frame her neck and found purchase as he cupped her face in his large hands. She dropped her arms to let the robe slip to the floor. She then brought them around him and up his back to pull him close and feel the contours of his chest against hers. They were both aware of the other's heart beating a strong and steady tattoo in a rhythmic duet. Andy lowered his head. Judy instinctively rose to meet him. Their joining was electric. Andy wanted to be slow and gentle; but the power coming from Judy demanded to be met. The music changed to a deep grinding guitar, mirroring their passion. Andy picked her up and brought her to the bed. His mind screamed to be aware of her and to follow her lead. He kissed her eyes closed as her lay beside her.

She turned to him. "Keep me close, Andy. Please don't pull away. I need to feel you and know it's you."

"Sure, baby. Sure." He drew her to him and touched her slowly. At first, he thought she might feel better if her eyes were closed but he said, "Look at me Judy. Keep your eyes on me, okay?"

"Okay."

He faltered at her haunted look. He knew so much was at stake. He started at her face and made love to her body, talking to her with quiet gentle words of the love he had for her and what he hoped for them. He was amazed that she should love him back and took pride in calling her his own.

Judy knew she had to make the final move because Andy would not, no matter what it cost him. The fact that she had no qualms about pulling him to her was the final glorious release from a life of fear.

Judy awoke first. She wasn't startled awake as she had been from nightmares. She woke with the knowledge that she would never feel being a victim again, and she smiled.

That was the first thing Andy saw when he opened his eyes. He imprinted that smile into his brain and knew he had found his new happy place.

She looked up at him and said, "Yes."

He understood and pulled her tighter. "Start packing."

Mrs. Gage was thrilled for something to distract from her meltdown. She pulled Kenann and Granny James aside. "I am happy to share this news. Andy and Judy are on their way to Las Vegas to get married."

"That's awesome!" Kenann squealed. "Did they just call? What did they say? Judy sound okay."

"She sounded wonderful. I think we can stop worrying about our Judy. She has found her safe home."

Granny smiled. "I couldn't be happier. When will we be seeing them?"

"Our next stop was to be London. I may send them ahead for an impromptu working honeymoon. Our next move will depend on what happens here."

"Won't that be Carter's call?" Granny asked

"Idiot," Mrs. Gage spat. Then she offered apologetically, "I'm sorry."

Kenann ventured, "Are you okay, Mrs. G?"

"I am so sorry for my behavior. Quite uncharacteristic of me, to say the least. I pride myself in having a cool head."

"Mrs. G, Jake and Carter are feuding over you."

Mrs. Gage's face gave nothing away. "Not my concern," was all she offered. "Okay, let us reconvene and share our good news and get down to business."

Everyone played nice as they hashed out the details of their plan. Carter and Jake sat as far away from each other as possible. They agreed with Kenann that a little "field trip" was in order and incorporated it into the master plan. Carter updated them on the data that Judy and Andy had been able to compile and send to Langley. They were slowly building the profile that they needed about the current society. Mrs. Gage asked Carter if he had had a chance to review the notes provided by the others in the group.

"Preliminary impressions are these: in some cases, it appeared the society was instrumental in promoting movements and regimes as in the case of the Nazis. Their trademark of mind control and extortion is all over that bunch. In the case of Rome and the Babylonian empires, they infiltrated an existing and relatively healthy regime and poisoned it for their own means. They either recruit or place their own people into key positions and impact policy and decisions."

Granny whispered to Danny Mac, "I'll bet Mordecai was one of theirs." Danny nodded, thinking of the book of Esther in the Bible.

Jake asked, "What's their endgame?"

Angelo spoke up. He remained so quiet they forgot he was even there. "They are not unlike any secret society. They have a very few powerful people at the top who perpetuate their power. They get off on controlling the *mindless masses*."

Danny Mac offered, "But you have to give them some credit for being able to maintain their identity as a single entity for such a length of time. That has taken some pretty amazing organizational skills and power."

Jake added, "Compare that to God's people, Danny Mac."

Carter rolled his eyes. "Oh, here we go." Everyone ignored him.

Granny chimed in, "Absolutely, Jake. From the beginning of time, there has been a consistent message and path provided and directed by God. And it has played out down through the ages and in history."

Carter continued, "Oh, come on. The next thing I know, you will be saying the boogeyman Satan is behind this society." All eyes were on him, but no one spoke. He looked from one to the other. "You can't be serious!"

Danny Mac said, "If you believe in God—and we do—you have to believe in Satan. You can't have good without evil."

"Whatever. I'm not going to turn this into some holy war. Let's just stick to the task at hand."

"Agreed." Mrs. Gage stood. "Who is taking the next shift on the monitors? Johnson needs a break. He has been on duty for several hours."

Danny Mac offered, "Kenann and I will. The rest of you get some sleep. Jake wants me to wake you at...say, three?"

"Sounds good."

Johnson was happy to get out of the dark room with its bank of monitors. Danny Mac ordered him to get some rest then locked the door behind him. He turned to Kenann with a grin.

"Danny Mac?" Her voice held teasing admonishment.

"Hey, I'm a great multitasker. Now come here."

29

WHITTAKER HAD RECOVERED sufficiently to accompany Andy and Judy to Vegas for their wedding. Since both were federal agents, they were allowed to travel armed. They wasted no time but went straight to the chapel from the airport. It was decorated as an Italian villa overlooking the Mediterranean Sea. Judy was grinning from ear to ear as she repeated the vows. Andy spoke his vows with tender solemnity as he committed his life to this woman. *No one else. Forevermore.*

They checked into the Palace Hotel, making sure they had adjoining rooms. Despite their desire for privacy, the need for security and backup was never far from their thoughts. Their flight back to Memphis left at ten the next morning. Andy bid Whittaker a good night at their adjoining door.

Whittaker couldn't help himself. "I need a code word."

Andy raised an eyebrow. "Why?"

He leaned in and said conspiratorially, "Well I don't want to come in with guns blazing just because I hear some hollering."

Andy tried to look stern as he closed the door. "Good night, Whittaker."

"Good night, sir."

"What was that all about?" Judy asked as she came out of the bathroom.

"Oh, just shop talk."

"No shop talk tonight, mister."

"Yes, boss."

"We are married."

"Yes, we are, Mrs. O'Hanlon."

"Hey, you need to meet my parents."

"It wouldn't be a bad idea."

"Kenann sure shook up all our lives, didn't she?"

"Well, the combination of Danny Mac and Kenann did, I'd say."

"Are you happy?"

Andy opened his arms to her. "Come on over here and see what you think."

The next morning, the crew met at the long table. For expediency, all the women were under the full covering of burqas. Danny Mac and Angelo wore kufiyas and sunglasses. Since they were the only men dark enough to make it convincing, they were leading the contingency of women. They planned to split up. Danny and David Angelo both spoke Arabic so they would each lead a group. Angelo and Mrs. Gage would take facial recognition cameras to the airport to see if they could catch any activity. Danny Mac, Kenann, and Granny would monitor the activity around the house. Unfortunately, this left Jake and Carter to their own devices.

Danny Mac confronted them both. "We have a job to do, men. I know that and you know that. When I come back, I expect you two to have worked out the outline of our counterattack from here. Understood?"

"Understood," they responded in stone-faced unison.

The others entered their vehicles with David Angelo and Mrs. Gage in the lead. Their escape route led them to the property of an unoccupied estate. They emerged from the tunnel unseen by anyone. They then entered mainstream traffic from the gates of this second estate and would return to their hideaway in the same manner. Danny Mac and his crew were able to find a bazaar close by with a clear view of the house. They set about milling through the crowd with an eye to surveillance. David Angelo and Mrs. Gage set up at the international arrival gate and began feeding the information to the techs in Langley.

Meanwhile, back at the underground compound, silence ruled. Johnson sat at the table with the schematics of the house in front of him. He heard the same request as the other men: Devise a plan to harass the invaders. He was not going to chastise his boss, and he sure as hell was not going to beg him to help. So he unrolled the tube and got down to work on his own.

30

ANGELO AND MRS. Gage were talking quietly while their surveillance camera operated. Angelo suddenly froze in place.

"What is it, David?"

He did not respond for a few seconds. "See those men coming through customs now?" She nodded. "They are the forward guards for the order. They always go before the leadership to secure the area."

"Well then, let us ensure we pay close attention to who follows them, shall we?"

Several people flowed through who did not appear to fit their expectations; but they recorded them nonetheless. The aforementioned men panned out around the perimeter as one would expect. Finally, several men approached the gate. They appeared to be walking in formation. It was not until they turned the corner to the gate that they saw the guards were flanking a man in a wheelchair. The man raised his head to speak through his assistive device.

"Oh sweet Lord!" Mrs. Gage gasped.

"This is not good. This is not good at all."

Kenann was enjoying herself at the bazaar. She could almost understand why women might wear such a covering. She felt such anonymity. It was rather liberating, really. She made her way to the entrance of the house they were supposed to be enjoying. She wanted to get as close as possible so as not to miss any clue that might be helpful. She was not mindful that she had wandered from the others until she turned back to speak quietly to Mrs. Gage and found herself surrounded by a group of school children. She looked around for the others but could not make them out in the crowd. Even Danny Mac was not discernible from the other men in Kafiyahs. A woman tried to speak to her; but she simply shook her head and moved further away. The children began chattering to her excitedly. She was becoming disoriented. She could not understand them or why they had turned their attention to her. Once again, she looked frantically around for Danny Mac. What she couldn't know was Danny Mac had begun looking frantically for her on the other side of the complex. Kenann had made her way to the opposite side of the bazaar, and the noise of the city obscured the drama playing out several feet from him.

Kenann was surrounded now by children and women yelling at her as they began pulling on her burqa. She tried to evade their grasps to no avail. One woman shoved her, knocking her to the ground. The children tore the burqa from her. Once her face was revealed, the clamor escalated. She scrambled to her feet and fled. The women and children pummeled her with stones from the roadway. One struck her on the side of the head as she ran, sending her stumbling into the stone wall flanking the road. She regained her footing and ran on, afraid to look back. Blood poured from her head wound, obscuring her vision. She wiped at it frantically as she ran, afraid she would be overtaken. Finally, she stepped into an alley to get her bearings. She was separated from Danny Mac and Granny with no phone, no money, and no papers. She was not even sure what street she had taken during her flight. If she returned to the bazaar, would she be attacked again? What she had done to be attacked eluded her. Obviously, they had realized she was an imposter in her traditional garb. Whatever the reason, she was in deep trouble.

She finished wiping the blood from her eyes and decided she had no choice but to find her way back to the bazaar. She had to get back to Danny Mac. She looked down and saw the small blood droplets she had shed as she ran and followed them back to the road that finally looked familiar and began to feel a glimmer of hope that all would be fine. She was vaguely aware of an incoming vehicle slowing as it approached. A black sedan pulled up in front of her. The window rolled down silently.

A breathless mechanical voice said, "Hello, Inanna."

31

ANGELO POCKETED HIS small surveillance camera and told Mrs. Gage, "Come on, we have to follow them."

"We know where they are going, David Angelo."

Angelo smirked. "Yeah, I guess you are right."

Mrs. Gage continued, "But this certainly changes things a bit. We need to rendezvous with the others and decide our next move. I don't want to discuss this over the phone with Daniel. Let's call them in, and we will return to our operation's base."

Angelo wondered how and why this petite little woman thought and acted like a military leader. They made their way to their vehicle as Angelo called Danny Mac.

Danny Mac was breathless when he answered, "Angelo, Kenann is missing."

"What? What happened?"

"I don't know. I looked away for a few minutes and then when I turned back, she was gone. All I could see were those damn burqas everywhere."

Angelo took note that this was the first time he had heard the new Danny Mac curse. "Is Mrs. James with you?"

"Yes."

"Where are you now?"

"At a bazaar in front of the house."

"Stay there. We're on our way."

Angelo and Mrs. Gage wasted no time in coming. While Mrs. Gage stayed with Granny, Danny Mac and Angelo began inquiring if anyone had seen anything amiss. It took a few minutes, but they were finally able to piece together what happened. Apparently, as Kenann looked intently for Danny Mac, she was reprimanded by a woman for not following the tradition of *ghadd al-basar* (lowering the eyes). When she shook her head and walked away, the women became enraged and charged the children to defend the prophet. One man was able to point in the direction Kenann fled as she was pursued by the children and women.

Danny Mac and Angelo ran back to the women to inform them of what had transpired when the caravan of sedans pulled into the driveway of the house. They pulled up to the portico in turns to dislodge the passengers out of the sight of the onlookers.

Danny Mac voice was steel. "I'm going after Kenann."

"I'll go with you," Angelo said.

"No, take the women back to the shelter."

Angelo did not argue; but as Danny Mac was ready to bolt, he touched his arm. "You need to know, my friend. Pierre was in that vehicle."

"I know."

Angelo did not question how he knew.

Jake jumped up from the monitor. He bent over to get a better look. His instinct was to run out of the room and get someone;

but he knew he had to pay close attention and record each detail of what was playing out in front of him.

It did not take Danny Mac long to track Kenann's blood from the place where she took the hit on her head. He was able to determine the spot she stopped to gain her bearings and that she too had followed her own trail back. He could now distinguish the difference in the blood spatter on her return journey. His blood ran cold as he saw the spatter on the roadway and knew it was where she had been forced into a vehicle. He began to run. He did not stop to think but ran through the gate and up to the door of the villa. He began pounding on the heavy door. It was opened by a large man in a suit who merely stepped aside as Danny Mac ran in.

The man spoke, "She is in this room," and gestured with his arm. Danny Mac ran through the door and found Kenann sitting quietly in a chair, staring straight ahead. He ran and knelt in front of her.

"Are you okay, baby?"

She did not answer but he caught the glint in her eye, and he knew. She was playing at something. He had only to go along. He put his hands on her shoulders and shook her slightly, "Answer me. What did they do to you? Are you okay?"

From behind him, Danny heard the sound of mechanical laughter and whirled on his heels. Pierre rolled into the room, strapped into a wheelchair powered by a breathing tube. His face was contorted as he tried to control his own saliva. He wheezed, gurgled, and then spoke through another device attached to his chair.

"This exceeds my own expectations. The gods have favored me with not one, but two sacrifices for my enjoyment."

"Crazy as ever, I see."

"Oh, you have no idea the depths to which my madness can go, but you shall soon see. Inanna knows she has been a bad girl and must be punished. The shock of seeing me has rendered her helpless. Just the way I like her. Even though you stole her virginity from me, I shall steal her soul from you."

"Pierre, I am warning you—"

"Warning *me*?" His maniacal laughter filled the room. Its mechanical nature did nothing to dispel the chilling effect.

32

JAKE HEARD WHAT was left of the group return and left his post long enough to open the door and usher them in. They gathered around his chair as he related what he had seen. Carter was peeved that Jake had not contacted him sooner but he figured he had that coming. What Mrs. Gage had said hit him to his core. He no longer had the power of the Pentagon behind him. This group cared not one whit about his combat action ribbons or his connections in Congress. He had better fall in line or fall out.

Angelo filled in the group about Kenann's attack in the bazaar and Danny's pursuit of her. They surmised he had somehow figured out what happened and went into the lion's den to get her. Unfortunately, the rooms above were not all wired for audio so they were forced to interpret what they were seeing on screen.

Pierre appeared to be giving a long discourse. Kenann appeared to be in shock. Danny Mac continued to kneel next to her and hold her hand.

Judy and Andy had finished packing for their trip to London as the advance operating party when Whittaker knocked on their door.

"You are needed, sir."

Andy looked at Judy whose heart fell to her feet. He followed Whittaker to the small secure command center Mrs. Gage had on the third floor. Mrs. Gage's diminutive form filled the screen on the monitor.

"I'm sorry, Andrew, but you and Judy will be needed here."

"What is it Mrs. G.? Give it to me straight."

"Pierre has Danny and Kenann."

"Shit!"

"Exactly."

"We will be on the next flight. You can brief me then. Are they okay?"

"So far."

"We will hurry."

Whittaker was instructed by Carter to stay put. That rankled, but he obeyed orders. He and CJ drove Judy and Andy to the airport.

"Watch after the kid."

"You got it," CJ said.

Whittaker wanted so badly to be on that plane. "Boss?"

"Yeah?" Andy answered.

"Bring them back, okay?"

"Count on it."

Everyone had left the room except Jake, who continued to watch the monitors, and Mrs. Gage, who had just finished her call to Andy.

"Gabrielle—"

"Jacob, don't."

"Hear me out. I have been a widow for several years. She was the only one, you know."

"I understand, Jacob. I should never have said such a spiteful and ugly thing to you."

"You misunderstand, Gabrielle. I'm rusty." He grabbed her hand, pulling her onto his lap. Cradling her like a child, he kissed her with all the passion of his youth.

33

JAKE RAISED HIS head. Mrs. Gage was very still in his arms, eyes closed. Jake was quite satisfied in her response to his kiss. He waited.

With eyes still closed, she finally said, "It has been a very long time since I have been that surprised." She slowly opened her eyes to his and smiled.

Jake released her to stand by his chair. "Well, it won't be the last." He took her shoulders and turned her around. He then swatted her on the behind.

She jumped and moved toward the door, looking over her shoulder with a smile. Smoothing her hair before reaching for the door, she remembered the recent events, and her face took on a steely determination as she opened the door. "All right, ladies and gentlemen. Council of war." She signaled her butler to assume monitoring duties. She leaned in as he passed, "Come get us at the slightest change."

They gathered around the table.

Granny spoke first. "Can't we just go get them through the panels?"

Jake explained, “We can and we will, Moira, but we must use this to our advantage first. If we show our hand too quickly, they will realize the panels are there despite no obvious openings and take axes to the walls if they have to.”

“But won’t they just find the false basement?”

“That is the idea but—”

“Come quickly, Mrs. Gage.”

She jumped up; as did the rest of the group. She saw immediately why Biggs had raised the alarm. Danny Mac and Kenann were being forced into the waiting cars.

Carter took control. “Come on, Angelo, get me out of here and after those cars.”

They wasted no time. Angelo went airborne as he exited the tunnel. Since the outlet was so far from the original house, they held little hope of getting eyes on to follow. Mrs. Gage told Angelo they had turned right out the gate and assumed they were returning to the airport. Angelo headed there and prayed they were right. With their current speed, they hoped they would arrive first and position themselves strategically to observe incoming vehicles. They soon breathed a little easier. They saw them ahead of them. Angelo put two cars between them but had to break away when they were admitted to a restricted zone.

“What do we do now, Mrs. Gage?”

“They are securing private transport. Stand down until I make some calls.”

She called him back in about ten minutes. “They have secured a small jet with a crew of five. I am still working on their flight plan. Angelo, go into the airport and get as close to that private terminal as you can. I believe there is a nice vantage point from the KLM waiting room. As soon as you are there, report back in. Mr. Carter, stay with the car. If Angelo needs to make a hasty exit, you can pull up to the front and pick him up. Agreed?”

“Roger that.” Carter looked at Angelo and rolled his eyes.

Angelo grinned and exited the vehicle. Once he was in place, he called Mrs. Gage, who promptly connected them to Carter via the car's bluetooth.

"What are you seeing, David Angelo?"

"There is not much activity. Wait…I see what they have done. There are three people in wheelchairs being boarded on the jet. Any word on their destination?"

"Not yet. I don't want to jeopardize the integrity of my man in place at the airport by asking him to be nosey. He will get the information, but he has to be circumspect. Do you have any contacts we might be able to utilize, Mr. Carter?"

"Can you patch me through on this thing?"

"Certainly."

He gave her a number in the Pentagon. When they answered, he gave his identifying numbers and was instructed to state the nature of his call. He was put through to his colleague at one of the military bases in Turkey. He provided some vague details of his needs and requested the flight manifest for a private plane leaving the airport now. Angelo was able to read off the tag number for the aircraft. Carter warned that discretion was of the utmost importance. The flight crew or anyone associated with the flight could know they were being investigated. They waited on the line while the man searched for the information.

"Hunting vampires now, Carter?" the man asked with a chuckle.

"What the hell are you talking about?"

"Your plane is going to a small airstrip in Brasov, Romania. That's Transylvania, my friend."

34

ONCE AGAIN, THEY were sitting around the main table in the hidden shelter. They had discussed going back up to the main house; but no one wanted to go. Mrs. Gage did allow the staff to return where there were better facilities for preparing meals.

"I've contacted my friends in Romania. They will have several people on standby at the airport in Brasov. They will follow them and see where Danny and Kenann are taken and be able to report to us."

"Shouldn't we be going?" Granny asked.

"We will, my dear. But I need time to secure transport, lodgings, and see to other logistical factors."

"I'm sorry Gabrielle. I'm just fretful. And I don't need to be. Those kids are in God's hands. He will take care of them."

If anyone noticed Carter's eye-rolling, they did not acknowledge it.

"Since Judy and Andy were changing planes in Vienna, I have instructed them to stay there while we regroup. There is no need for them to come here when we will be leaving soon ourselves. I have made accommodations for them in the bridal suite at a lovely hotel near the park and asked them to consider it a wedding present."

"He's on duty, madam. Did you consider consulting his *boss* before you planned his schedule?"

"Do you want him to travel here?"

"Well, no."

"Do you need him to be somewhere else?"

"Well, not right now."

"Do you have a problem with me footing the bill for their lodging?"

"All right, you've made your point. But I would appreciate being consulted."

"The same way you consulted me in Memphis?"

Carter opened his mouth to rebut and was unable to come up with a plausible comeback. Everyone had held their peace during this exchange, knowing Mrs. Gage would more than hold her own.

When Carter remained quiet, Mrs. Gage continued but with a more deferential tone, "What are our suggestions for the next steps?"

Carter looked as if he was going to remain silent. But then his countenance changed, and he began to contemplate. No one interrupted him. Finally, he spoke. "Angelo has confirmed that Pierre remains at the head of the order in light of his protection by the presidential guard, if you will. So, once again, we have been able to infiltrate the top echelon."

"I would hardly call abduction an infiltration," Jacob countered.

"The end results are the same."

"If we had planned to do that, we would have sent them in with comm devices."

"And if we had, they would have been discovered in the first ten minutes. The last time Danny and Kenann were in their hands, they had no reason to search them. They won't make that mistake again. This serves our purposes nicely." If Carter felt the animosity in the room, he chose to ignore it. He continued, "Danny and Kenann are resourceful. They will hold their own till the cavalry arrives. Our next task is to establish a base camp near enough to work, but not so near as to arouse suspicion."

"I'm way ahead of you on that, Mr. Carter." Mrs. Gage smiled at him.

"I had no doubt, madam." He allowed himself to smile back. A tentative truce was being formed. "What have you arranged?"

"Since we have been speaking, I received a text as to where the kids have been taken. It is a castle high in the mountains above Brasov. A private residence, no doubt owned by the order. My staff took the liberty of securing a resort chalet nearby. The Carpathian mountains of Transylvania are becoming known for their skiing and winter sports activities. I will have snow mobiles and all-terrain vehicles on site as well as a private helicopter for surveillance."

"Excellent. Perfect. We can scour the hills under the guise of tourists. And once we have a firm plan in place, someone will need to be captured so we can inform Danny."

All voices rang in unison, "I'll do it!"

Carter was both intrigued and uncomfortable at the loyalty and love this group held for each other. They were all talking at once, building their case for why they should be the one to go.

"Enough!" he commanded. "We will decide that at a later date. First, we must have a plan to pass on to him. That will best be developed once we have the lay of the land. Agreed?"

All consented.

Andy and Judy made their way through the picturesque streets of Vienna. Andy asked the cab driver to make a stop at St. Stephens Cathedral along the Danube. He had always loved that area of the city with its beautiful bridges and architecture. The cathedral filled the sky above them as they looked up from the plaza before it.

Judy marveled at the view. "It was so sweet of Mrs. Gage to do this for us."

"Yeah. I bet Carter had a fit."

"Screw Carter."

"Judy!"

"I'm sorry. He gets under my skin."

"Well, he is your husband's boss, so play nice."

"My husband." She smiled up at him.

He returned her smile. "Let's go get some ice cream. I know this great little shop that sells Italian Eis across the bridge."

He paid the cab driver and dismissed him. They held hands across the wide bridge reveling in the early fall day in Vienna.

"I can't believe that hotel suite. I will never stay in anything so posh again," Judy gushed.

"Not on my salary." Andy laughed.

"Well, once I get another job, we should do okay."

"Do you want to work?"

"Are you kidding? That is all I know. If you turn me into a *hausfrau*, I shall become psychotic and put arsenic in your cornflakes."

"A job it is then." They both laughed.

Judy sobered. "I assume we will live in DC? Is your place big enough for me too?"

"It should be. If not, we will look for one together. That would be fun. It may depend on where you decide to work. Hey, we may even move to the burbs."

"I'm excited, Andy. And I haven't been excited in a long time."

"Oh, really?" He raised an eyebrow.

Judy laughed. "You know what I mean. I'm starting to really live again and I like it. Even worrying about Danny Mac and Kenann doesn't take this joy away."

"We'll get them back, baby."

"I know. I know we will. Our little band of misfits is a force to be reckoned with."

They continued to stroll through the tree lined streets, stopping to explore some little shop or another. They jumped on the trolley that circles the city and got off at Freud's house, just so Judy could say she had seen it. They made their way to the park where live music was playing.

"Dance with me, Judy." He swept her into his arms as she laughed. They moved to a Viennese waltz on the cobblestones of the square.

"My beauty, my bride."

"My hero, my pain in the ass." He laughed at her.

"Well, I can tell who will be the romantic in this family."

"Yes, it may take a while for the Ice Princess to thaw."

"I'd say you are doing just fine." He gave her a devilish grin.

They had dinner at a cozy restaurant near the hotel. Afterward, he carried her over the threshold of their room despite her protests.

"How long are you going to do that?"

"As long as I can."

"You are goofy."

"Goofy over you."

"I can see it now. I'll come home with an armload of groceries, and you'll be trying to pick me up at the door."

"Absolutely! Or a baby on your hip."

Judy stopped and looked at him. "You want kids?"

"Don't you?"

"Well, I guess. I just figured you for the carefree no-kids type."

"Falling in love changes a man, Judy." He was dead serious, and she knew it.

Blade asked CJ if he wanted to come to his house. Since he was keeping close tabs on the kid, he thought that would be a good idea.

"Can I bring, Freddie?"

"Sure, Rough likes him."

They came up the walk from the alley to the back door.

"Mommm?"

A short olive-skinned woman came to the door, drying her hands on a dishtowel. "And who is this you brought home with you, little man?"

"This is my friend, CJ Baer. He is a friend of Mrs. Gage. Can he stay for dinner?"

"Sorry to intrude, Ma'am. Nice to meet you."

"You are welcome here. Come in, come in." She held the door wide open and stepped aside for them to enter. The home was modest but clean and cozy. She led the way into the dining room. "You are just in time for some soup and a sandwich. Hope that's okay."

"That will be fine. If you're sure it's no bother."

"Not at all."

"Mom, CJ is a truck driver. He has been all over the United States and Canada."

"How interesting! And who is this creature riding on your shoulder?"

"That is Freddie, Mom. He and Rough have made friends. Where is Rough?"

"Standing guard, as usual. I declare that dog is always on the alert. I can't imagine who he's looking out for."

When she turned her back, CJ winked at Blade and he smiled. Blade called for Rough, and he bounded into the room to receive his head rub. While Blade ruffled Rough's fur, Freddie climbed down from CJ's shoulders and sat on his lap. Rough came over and sniffed at Freddie, whose paw reached for the top of Rough's head. Rough's tail beat against Blade's leg in pleasure.

While they ate, CJ learned how Blade's mom and dad met in the Philippines when his father was stationed there. She returned with him to the States, and they had settled in his hometown of Memphis when he was discharged. He worked for a shipping company until he developed sickle-cell anemia and finally succumbed to it three years ago. Blade had been lost till Danny Mac came by and asked if they would like to come to his church. That friendship had saved Blade. He was once again a happy child, full of energy and life.

"I still can't believe he stowed away on Mrs. Gage's plane last summer. But he certainly had a nice vacation out of it."

Once again, Blade and CJ exchanged smiles while Mrs. served the soup and sandwiches. Little did she know her son helped foil a plot of international terrorists. He was just a fifth grader who also happened to know the phone number of a top level CIA operative.

Mrs. Daniels began tidying up the dishes. "So tell me about yourself, Mr. Baer."

"Not much to tell. Been trucking all my adult life."

"Do you have family?"

"I've got a brother and two sisters, but we don't see each other much. Usually around Christmas."

"Where is home?"

"My truck."

"Seriously. No wife or children?"

"Nope. Just me and Freddie and my Peterbilt."

"Well, you must feel free to stop by any time you're in town."

"Thank you, Ma'am. I'm doing a little work for Mrs. Gage right now, so I will be around awhile."

"Well then, you must not be a stranger."

"Since Danny Mac is gone for awhile, me and CJ are gonna hang out together."

"Where has Danny Mac gone?"

"He is doing some mission work for the church. Mrs. Gage is helping him since she has so much money."

CJ was amazed at how easily this story rolled from Blade's lips. Maybe he had a career in the spy business after all.

Kenann had feigned hysteria upon being taken into the mansion in Istanbul. When Danny Mac arrived, she was in a full-blown catatonic state. Her intention was to keep her captors off-balance. She knew Pierre would try to work on her mind and break her down. If she was already *crazy*, he would have nothing to work with.

Danny Mac knew immediately that she was playing a part. The flicker of a glance his way told him to play along. He knelt in front of her. "Kenann, what's wrong, baby? Are you all right?" He looked back over his shoulder. "Pierre, what have you done to her?"

His laughter came out in raspy bursts of air. "Apparently, seeing me again was too much for her."

"We know you hypnotized her.'

"Yes, it was so enjoyable playing with her mind."

"And now you have broken her altogether. She was already so fragile."

"Daniel, you have seen nothing of what I can do to her. Take them away."

When they approached Kenann, she began to snarl and lunged at the men. She bared her teeth and snapped at their hands as they tried to grab her. The men backed off and turned to Pierre. "Boss?"

Danny took the opportunity. "Let me try."

He approached her slowly as if she were a dangerous animal. "Kenann? You need to come with me now."

She pulled back but made eye contact. She jerked back again as he reached for her.

"Kenann, you come with me, okay?"

She let him take her hand; but she maintained a wary expression. Danny Mac turned to Pierre. "Where do you want us to go? I need to stay with her. In this state, it's hard to tell what she will do."

Pierre hesitated briefly before commanding, "Go."

Danny Mac put a solicitous arm around Kenann. Walking behind the men, he put his lips to her ear and whispered, "Bravo."

Mrs. Gage had all assembled and settled into their chalet in a high mountainous vale of the Carpathian's overlooking Brasov. Judy and Andy had arrived that afternoon and had been brought up to speed by Carter. Granny and Mrs. Gage had embraced Judy warmly at the airport, congratulating her on her marriage.

Judy's cheeks turned pinked as she smiled demurely. "I've never been happier."

"That's wonderful, dear."

"Yes, sweetheart. We are so pleased for you."

"Now"—Judy got down to business—"what's the plan to get Kenann and Danny Mac back?"

Mrs. Gage replied, "We are going to play tourists and do recon through the woods. Then once we have the plan established, one of us will get taken by the brutes and fill Danny and Kenann in on the plan."

"Sounds good. Want to go down into the village and snoop around?" Judy asked.

"Excellent. Moira, feel like a bit of shopping?"

"Absolutely!"

"Good, then I shall go and get us some head scarves and sunglasses to avoid knowing eyes." Mrs. Gage checked in with the men as to their destination.

Andy offered to accompany them but was reassured they would be fine. They would stay in busy public places. When Mrs. Gage produced a pistol from her purse, Andy laughed and relented.

The women took the roadster down into town. The cold air took their breath; but they laughed and enjoyed the shared experience. In their chic headscarves and designer sunglasses, they looked every bit the "smart set." They roamed through the shops, listening for conversations that might glean some nugget of information.

They had just emerged from a jewelry store when Mrs. Gage exclaimed, "Nita, darling!" She turned slightly. "Pinky? What in the world are you two doing here?"

Nita was tall and lithe with lustrous red hair; she exuded sex appeal. Pinky was blond and cute and seemed happy *just to be there.*

Nita offered, "We are on a bit of a holiday, Gabby dear. We both just needed to get a way. Take a break, you know?"

"Yes, darling. I do indeed."

Pinky chimed in, "What brings you to this backwater place?"

"Oh, this and that. You know how it is." The women all grinned at each other. "Oh, but where are my manners! These are my friends, Judy and Moira."

Greetings were made all around. Mrs. Gage looked at her old friends and decided. "Where are you staying?"

Pinky answered, "We have a nice little flat with a view of the mountains."

"Come stay with me." Judy and Granny both whipped their heads to stare with intent at Mrs. Gage.

Nita touched Mrs. Gage's arm. "That is so sweet, Gabby, but our accommodations are fine."

"I insist and absolutely will not take no for an answer."

Pinky became effusive. "*Oooh!* I know you have some great digs. Where are you?"

Mrs. Gage pointed up into the mountains. "I think you will like it. Now go get your things together. Do you have your own vehicle?" They nodded. "Good, I will come by and you can follow me."

They provided her with the address and directions and went off arm in arm, giggling together. As soon as they were out of ear shot, Judy and Granny pounced.

"What are you doing?"

"We can't entertain guests at a time like this."

"My darlings, Nita's real name is Briget. Her *nom de plume* was given to her by some friends of ours. Nita stands for Notorious International Terrorist Armoire." She laughed.

Kenann had kept up her ruse throughout the journey to the castle in Transylvania. Once there and placed in a bedroom overlooking the valley below, Danny Mac began searching a means of escape. He went out on the balcony and to his dismay, found it to hang over a cliff of indeterminate depth descending into darkness. When he came in, he saw Kenann crawling around on her knees near the fireplace. He went to her and helped her up, whispering in her ear "What are you doing?"

She whispered back, "I'm ready for my close up, Mr. Deville."

She used the cover of their bodies in a loose embrace to apply the ashes from the fireplace under her eyes. It made her look more crazed than before. She began to keen and pull at her curly disheveled hair. Danny Mac knew this was part of her efforts to look the part of a woman who had gone completely out of her mind. They both were working off the assumption that they were under video surveillance and only spoke in close whispers.

"Is the door locked?" she whispered as she made a pacing pass by Danny Mac.

She had taken to mumbling to herself as she walked around to cover the occasions when she spoke to Danny Mac. He subtly raised one finger in yes. They had prearranged hand signals on the flight over from Istanbul. Eventually, they heard the sound of a key in the lock. She scurried over and cowered in a corner.

One of Pierre's men entered with a food tray. "Boss wants to meet with you two after dinner." He laid the tray on a side table and left.

Danny Mac spoke in conciliatory tones. "Come on over here, Kenann. You need to eat."

She came slowly and sat, her wary eyes never leaving Danny Mac. He fixed her a plate and sat it in front of her. She paused a few seconds and then attacked the food, shoveling it into her mouth with her hands. Danny Mac had to exercise great control to keep from laughing. He was so proud of her deceptive skills. *A good quality to have in a wife*, he thought.

Several minutes later, they were escorted to Pierre's apartment. It was an amalgam of hospital room and a command center. Danny Mac took the opportunity to observe Pierre's condition. He was obviously paralyzed from the neck down. He controlled his wheelchair through a breathing tube. He had lost all control over his body but apparently, continued complete control over the order.

Pierre turned to them. "This is what the two of you have reduced me to. You have no idea the depth of my desire for revenge." He had to stop several times in an attempt to control his spittle; but his words came out wet and mechanical, nonetheless.

"What do you want with us, Pierre?" Danny Mac asked as Kenann began to roam aimlessly around the room. The men gave her a wide berth, which was her desired intention.

"I want to hurt you!" Pierre spat.

"Okay, I get that. I'm the one who put you in that chair, but Kenann killed Katarina as a favor to you. As far as I know, you put it into her head when you hypnotized her. You and I both know you were going to finish her off anyway."

Pierre gave what was intended for a laugh. "Yes, I was."

"So you might as well let her go. I knew she was unstable. That is why I married her. It was my fault she got into that mess. I felt responsible and sorry for her." Even though she knew Danny Mac was trying to diminish Pierre's ability to control her, his words stung deeply.

Pierre hissed, "She is Inanna! She does not belong to you!"

At these words, Kenann came over and stood in front of Pierre. His men came to attention and moved closer. She simply stood and stared at him, vacantly tilting her head this way and that like a bird. Pierre returned her gaze, willing her to remember him as her consort. After a few moments, she moved away.

"See, Pierre? She's completely mad. No good to you any longer."

"Shut up! You're the one who is no longer of use to me."

Kenann responded instinctively. She ran over and grabbed Danny Mac's arm. Remembering her ruse, she then cowered behind his back and started keening. She dropped to the floor and wrapped her arms around his legs. Her wailing increased. She had to make Danny Mac necessary in keeping her calm. She had to make him valuable enough to keep alive. Danny Mac stroked her hair and the embrace of his legs increased.

Pierre observed this exchange with a steely glare. "I may need you now to care for Kenann, but that does not mean I cannot break you any time I chose as well." Kenann threw back her head and wailed. She started pulling her hair and pounding on the floor. "Get them out of here!" Pierre barked.

Danny Mac reached for her, and she allowed herself to be brought to her feet. She sniffed and mumbled incoherently as she shuffled away, holding on to Danny Mac. On the way back to their room, Kenann attempted to wander off to judge the reactions of their guards. She was pleased to see that they did not react swiftly to bring her back. They seemed afraid of her. She had ambled down an adjacent hallway, mumbling and touching various ornamentations and pictures on the wall before they shoved Danny Mac to bring her back. When they made it to their room,

Kenann put her back against the door when they tried to close and lock it. She snapped her teeth at them and snarled. The men stood by helplessly.

Danny Mac came to their rescue. "Listen, chaps. We cannot escape from this fortress anyway. Leave the door open so she will settle down. And if she wants to ramble around, she can't hurt anything. She is harmless if you leave her alone." The men seemed relieved and more than willing to leave her alone. Danny Mac led her to the chair and helped her sit. "They will leave the door open, don't worry. You can relax and not feel confined, okay? Is that it? Are you afraid of being locked in?"

She whimpered and nodded her head slightly. Danny Mac looked to the men; they looked at each other. One man shrugged his shoulders, and they walked away leaving the door open. Danny and Kenann both resisted the urge to look at each other in victory.

"You did WHAT?" Carter roared. Mrs. Gage stood firm, riding out his rage. "How in the hell do we know they aren't already attached to the order? I cannot believe you did this on your own volition, Gabrielle. I have given you a fair amount of leeway but in this, you have gone too far. You may have compromised the whole operation with this impulsive stunt."

"John, I have known and worked with both of these women for years. Despite their presentation, they are consummate professionals. Their personas are their best disguise. Nita is an expert in martial arts and demolition in addition to her seductive powers. Pinky's real name is Annabelle Morgan and married into a royal family from Monaco. Her husband has no idea she is a mathematician and logistical genius whose specialty is code breaking. He thinks of her as his sweet vacuous wife who enjoys parties and fashion."

"That's all well and good, but that does nothing to quell my concerns about their loyalty to our cause. They could easily hire their expertise out to the highest bidder. Don't you find it curious that you should just *happen* to run into them."

"Well then, isn't it to our advantage to keep them close and under our watchful eye?"

"This is on you, Gabrielle. If it goes south, it's on you." He turned and left her.

She allowed herself to doubt the wisdom of her actions. She had worked with these ladies on several occasions and had never questioned their integrity or loyalty to just causes. She sent up a silent prayer that she had not put her friends in jeopardy.

35

DINNER AROUND THE massive oak table in the formal dining room was beyond tense. No one wanted to bring up anything relating to Danny Mac and Kenann in the presence of Nita and Pinky. As this was the only thing they cared for or could focus on, it made for very stilted conversation.

Nita took it as long as she could. "Gabby, I appreciate your hospitality, but I think it would be best if Pinky and I went back to our rooms in town."

The fact that no one jumped to dissuade her said volumes. The silence dragged on. Pinky's large blue eyes went from face to face, trying to understand what was happening here.

Mrs. Gage sighed. "Ladies, you know what I do."

Carter spoke quietly but with authority, "Careful."

Mrs. Gage gave him a pointed look. "Trust me please, Mr. Carter." She turned to her two compatriots. "My friends have raised a concern, and one I must consider for the welfare of all."

Nita responded, "What is it, dear?" Pinky placed her glass of wine on the table and gave her undivided attention.

"I have to know why you both are here in this village at this time."

Pinky laughed. "We told you, Gabby, we are on holiday."

"No, Pinky. Gabby needs to know the truth." Pinky looked at Mrs. Gage and flushed. Nita continued, "I got a call from Vincenzo. You remember him?" Mrs. Gage nodded. "He was very worried about his son. He said he had distanced himself from the family and quit his job. He had his men run surveillance on his activities. It appeared he was providing muscle for an obviously wealthy man confined to a wheelchair."

Mrs. Gage took note that no one reacted to this news. They were becoming skillful operatives. Mrs. Gage responded, "So you agreed to check it out for Vincenzo and followed them here?"

Pinky interjected, "I'm sorry, Gabby. I've never lied to you before. I just thought we were going to keep our cover."

"That's fine, Pinky. Just make sure you never lie to me again. Understood?" Pinky swallowed hard and nodded. She understood the threat. Mrs. Gage turned again to Nita. "Has Vincenzo's son ever seen you or Pinky? Does he know about you?"

"No. As you know, Vincenzo is very protective of his family, especially his son. He kept his work secure from them. Why do you ask?"

"I'd like to table that till I have time to confer with my colleagues, if that is acceptable?'

Nita nodded. "Of course."

Pinky chimed in, "Anything you say, Gabby." Mrs. Gage gave her a reassuring smile. Pinky let out the breath she did not realize she was holding.

Jake realized that even these people seemed to view Gabrielle with authority. *Who was this woman?*

The group, sans Nita and Pinky, convened in the library beside a roaring fire. Mrs. Gage's staff always attended to their creature comfort. Granny was afraid she was getting too spoiled to go back to her little farm in West Virginia. She had not told Kenann, but she was very lonely there. The church people helped; but she missed these friends deeply when she was at her home. She had sold all her livestock and was leasing the ground to her neighbor to use. He had also agreed to keep an eye on the place anytime she was away. She was seriously considering a move to Memphis.

Jake leaned forward with his elbows on his knees and hands clasped. "All right, Gabrielle. What are you cooking up in that head of yours?"

She gave her signature enigmatic smile. "Well, I don't see why we should not take advantage of this boon we have been given." No one spoke so she continued, "What if we were able to insert one or both of the ladies into the castle? They are unknown to the men who surround Pierre and will not be connected to us in anyway. We can continue our surveillance and any other plans we had; but if they can pull it off, it will be a tremendous advantage, don't you think?"

Carter broke the silence. "How do you intend to *insert* them into the castle?"

His sarcasm was not lost on her. "As the saying goes, this is not their first rodeo, Mr. Carter. If agreed by all, I can have them work up a plan." She sought the input of the others by her gaze. After a few seconds pause, the others gave their agreement to exploring this plan. Carter was the only silent partner.

So be it, Mrs. Gage thought.

Andy pulled Judy into his arms when they returned to their room. "Judy, have you contacted your parents?"

She flushed. "Well, no. Why?"

"When do you plan to tell them you are married?"

"I don't know." She knew her voice sounded petulant.

"What's holding you back?"

She stepped from his arms and began to pace. "I don't know. What we have is so special. I don't want anyone else in my bubble right now. Is that so wrong?"

"Well, when you put it that way, no. But I thought you were embarrassed or ashamed of me…or of them?"

She came to him swiftly. "No, my parents are great. They really are. But I have kept them at arm's length for so long they are almost an afterthought. We will call them together. Will that make you feel better?"

"I suppose. Because I need to let my mom know too. She is going to hit the roof that I didn't involve her. But she will have to deal with it. Ever since Dad died, I have been her main focus."

"You haven't said much about your mom."

"Well, to be honest, I was afraid she would scare you off, and I was trying everything I knew to talk you into an *us*."

"Good grief! How bad is she?"

"Well, let's just say, I thank God you're a strong woman."

Kenann had successfully overcome the barrier of being restricted to her room. All of Pierre's security stayed out of her way. She had found a long white gown among the items in the clothespress in their room. She was especially unnerving as she roamed the halls throughout the night in this trailing white gown, keening and pulling at her hair. Danny Mac waited patiently in the room as she performed her recon. If she wandered too far afield, the guards escorted Danny Mac to her to bring her back. Pierre's guard was completely spooked by her.

She tried to impart the intel to Danny Mac she had gained during her rounds; but this proved difficult. On her latest foray, she found paper and pen, which she hid in the slit pocket of her gown. She used this cover to jot down some pertinent information for Danny Mac to review and analyze. There were armed guards at all points of entrance or egress. But there did not seem to be a large contingency of men. She guessed about ten to twelve in total. She was also able to determine the shift rotation of the guards. There was one room used as an armory. At any given time, there were several weapons left in stock. In the command center/medical complex that supported Pierre's extensive needs, she took a sidelong glance at the bank of monitors along one entire wall. She described what she saw in her notes to her husband. She ended by saying she loved him.

He smiled as he surreptitiously read this and risked a glance at her. His eyes told her what she needed to hear. He took great care not to show the notes as he burned them while putting another log on the wood fire. Danny Mac busied himself with exercise and reading. He was summoned each day to report to Pierre on Kenann's state. Pierre gave no indications of his plans. He appeared to be content simply to be in possession of them at this point. Danny Mac learned what happened in the days following the collapse of the order in that subterranean cavern in Egypt.

Pierre wanted Danny Mac to know that regardless of their efforts, they were ineffective in destroying the order. The first people on the scene of Katrina's death found Pierre barely clinging to life. There were state of the art emergency medical equipment and personnel on site. He was immediately intubated and mechanically ventilated to save his life. Thanks to Danny Mac, his snapped spinal cord was irreparable. As soon as he gained consciousness, Pierre apparently wasted no time in regaining control over the order. The force of his will and character left no room for dispute. That and the network of assassins he had on his payroll tended to keep everyone in line. He was also in command of the order's extensive financial holdings. This allowed him to call the shots. Danny Mac could tell that what happened to Pierre had completed his descent into madness. His henchmen gave nothing away; but Danny Mac suspected they knew it too.

Danny Mac sensed that Kenann was agitated after her last recon. Her fingers trembled as she slipped him a note. She saw him drop his head as he read it and knew he was uttering a prayer for divine help. Kenann made a decision and surreptitiously wrote another note. When he read it, he considered it at length, terrified to weigh in on the wrong side. Kenann knew he was in serious thought and gave him the time and space he needed. She didn't want to be wrong either.

36

JAKE FOUND MRS. Gage sitting alone in the back garden of the chateau. The weather was brisk but she did not seem to notice. He stood outside the door and simply watched her. What weight did she carry on those diminutive shoulders that she allowed no one to help her? As if sensing his presence, she turned and reached out her hand to him. That simple gesture stole his breath. He moved toward her, taking her hand in his.

"Gabrielle."

"I am quite the old poop, aren't I, love?"

He grinned. "Well, I won't deny it, but I can say it hasn't scared me off."

"Good. Don't give up on me, Jacob."

"Never."

She knew he meant it; that alone gave her the courage to move forward. He had not touched her again or even referenced what had occurred between them in Istanbul. He had branded her, that's how it felt. She smiled inwardly as she imagined that's how he saw it too. *This woman is mine.* And she was growing quite enamored with this old-fashioned idea. Who knew that she could be so traditional in her beliefs? She laughed out loud.

"It is so good to hear that sound, Gabrielle."

"Yes, and it is good to feel it. Mr. Carter has a nasty way of making me doubt myself."

"That's his job. Unfortunately, he is very good at it. He keeps us all sharp, whether we like it or not."

"I suppose so. I brought Nita and Pinky here on a whim. He was right. I could have jeopardized all of us."

"Every commander is capable of making a tactical error, dear. It is only the ones who refuse to acknowledge them or learn from them who are the fools."

"Now see, you lovely man, you soothe and warm my soul with your words." He touched her cheek. "And you're chilled to the bone. Come with me." He pulled her to her feet and led her down a path into a wooded area, where she saw a large outbuilding housing the all-terrain vehicles. He pulled the heavy door open as if it were paper and allowed her to enter first. It was warm inside the building, thanks to overhead heaters. He led her to a sitting area for vacationing guests who were scheduling their use of the equipment. Since Mrs. Gage had reserved the entire chateau, the staff waited for her orders inside the main building. He pulled her down beside him in an oversized arm chair.

She laughed. "Jacob, this is the second time you have pulled me into a chair with you."

"And as I told you before, it won't be the last." He looked down at her; his eyes speaking volumes. "I will be whatever you need for as long as you need it. No strings. I love you, Gabrielle."

She reached up, framing his rugged handsome face with her delicate hands. Then she shocked herself as she laid her head on his large solid chest, grabbing his shirt on either side of her face and began to sob.

Jake wrapped her in his strong reliable arms and let her cry out whatever was rending her spirit into these shreds. It took awhile for her to regain her composure.

"I'm afraid I have ruined your shirt." Jake's only response was a dismissive grunt. He stroked her hair and remained silent, waiting for her to offer him her inner thoughts.

She made a move to stand up. She did make eye contact and mumbled something about fixing her face as she made her way to the public restroom next to the sitting area. She returned a few minutes later with a freshly scrubbed face but did not resume her seat with Jake. To all the world, she looked like a small shy child as she sat across from him, afraid to tell the adult some deep secret. He waited. This had to be completely on her terms. She appeared to steel herself with a deep breath and began to look more like the strong determined woman he knew. She appeared to consider as he waited.

Finally, she squared her shoulders and spoke, "Jacob, your words, your feelings have undone me. They made their way to my heart like a skilled archer. *My* heart." She paused as if going back into deep thought. Jake did not move. She gazed off into a distant time and place. Jake saw emotions cross her face as she remembered. He had decided she wasn't ready when she began speaking again.

Almost to herself, she related, "My village in Hungary was small. I played in the woods with my friends. When we were little, we never knew about the problems with the communists. It was an ideal part of my memories. My father had been a professor. He was part of the Intelligentsia and lost his position in Budapest during a purge by the government. From that day till Papa died, he was watched. It took its toll on him and Mama. He told me later that she missed the city and what his position offered. One dreary afternoon on the year I turned fifteen, she walked into the lake. She just walked in over her head and never looked back. How does a person do that? Who does that?"

Once again, she was lost in her thoughts. "I ran away with my boyfriend. We headed straight for Budapest and started fighting the communists. It doesn't take Freud to figure out why. We lived hard and fast and loved each other with abandon. He died in the middle of Hosok Tere."

Jake said nothing; but she realized she had used the Hungarian name. She shook her head as if to clear the other language from her mind and said, "Heroes Square. We were a part of a small rebellion in the city. The *politzi* opened fire. He was hit in the chest and died in my arms." She whispered, "My first love." She took a deep breath in and out and finally looked at Jake. "I was angry and hurt and lost. I could have gone home to Papa. I didn't. I was young and lithe. I used my body to get what I wanted or needed. I began to run in some big circles. I met my husband in those circles. I don't want to talk about that now. Another time. I will Jacob, I promise. I want you to know all of it."

"It's fine, Gabrielle. We can stop and go back to the main house. You're already drained."

"No, I want to get through this as much as I can tonight."

"All right. How about I sit next to you?" He wanted to be near her.

"Please." He did but did not touch her. She continued, "My marriage was brutal in many ways. Another blow to my psyche. Probably the worst, to be honest. But he died, and I inherited his considerable wealth. It took me a long time to find myself and my purpose. That more than anything else is why I am so fiercely independent. I fought hard for who and what I am now. It scares me to think about going back to a place where I give my heart again." She turned and looked at him directly. "Can you understand that, Jacob?"

"I can't say I understand completely. I haven't been where you are. But I loved my Mary more than life. So I can understand when you are afraid to take your heart to those places again."

He got it close enough, she mused. "I have a lot of people who depend on me. I take my responsibilities very seriously. I guess what I am saying is, my life is not simply my own. I don't know anyone who could put up with all that."

"Do you trust me, Gabrielle?"

"Completely."

He knew she did not say this lightly. He was more pleased than he dared show her at that moment. "All I ask is you let me help you. I don't want to run your life or control you, Gabrielle. It's obvious you have a very large operation under your command. I don't want to get in your way. I want to help you or, at the very least, stand beside you."

"I'm a fool to keep you out of my work…and my life. I will cherish you and your help."

He grinned. "Wait, it's all legal, right?"

She gave him her signature enigmatic smile. "Mostly."

Danny Mac pulled the sheet from the cabinet as instructed and continued around the room gathering the designated accoutrements. He heard the shower shut off. He took the items to the bathroom door and entered.

Kenann saw his expression change as she stepped onto the bathmat from the shower. She gave him a shy smile as she used the oversized towel to dry her body. He stood with his back against the closed door and watched her. As she wound her hair into a smaller towel and tucked it tightly on her head, he laid his bundle on the counter and came to her. He encircled her face with his palms and pulled her to his lips. He poured all his passion and longing into that kiss. Her towel came undone, and her hair fell free. Danny Mac wrapped the damp strands around his fist. He pulled her head back and deepened the kiss. Breathless and shaken, they both clung to each other when Danny Mac lifted his head.

"I love you, Danny Mac." Her voice was muffled against his shoulder.

"I love you."

Kenann pulled back and asked, "Ready?"

He made a noncommittal sound. "I've been praying for protection over you. You are in His hands. That is the only way I can allow you to do this.

"Help me prepare, and let's get this thing finished."

A few minutes later, Inanna emerged wrapped in the soft white Egyptian cotton sheet. Gold braid from the drapes held it in place. Kenann had no product to tame her hair so she braided and wound it into an elegant chignon. Small wisps of hair framed her face. They wasted no time. Kenann knew if she did not move quickly, she would lose her nerve. She raised her chin and allowed the persona to infuse her to her marrow. Until this was finished, she was Inanna.

They entered the hallway. The closest guard did nothing to stop them. His mouth was agape as he saw the transformation from the mad woman to this regal creature. As prearranged, Kenann entered the command center first, followed by Danny Mac in attendance. The reaction from Pierre was more than anticipated. His eyes, the only part of his body that could react without mechanical assistance, flared in astonishment and excitement.

As Kenann paused regally a few paces from Pierre's chair, Danny Mac came from behind and knelt in front of Pierre, bowing low from the waist. "As your humble servant, I present to you, Inanna, your royal consort."

No one breathed. Even the contingency of guards could not guess how Pierre would react. Danny Mac uttered another prayer to the Creator of the universe for his grace and power that he and Kenann would prevail.

"Inanna, are you here to stay?"

"Yes, my Lord."

"What is your wish?" His mechanical ventilation could not hide his breathless anticipation.

"I desire to take my rightful place as ruler of my vast empire with you at my side." She believed he would only appreciate someone who shared his desire for power. The gleam in his eyes confirmed her hunch.

"Come stand with me and allow me to show you what I have accomplished in your absence."

She moved beside him her moves fluid. In order to cement Danny Mac's position, she made herself touch Pierre's shoulder. "My dear, Daniel has been a faithful servant. I have awakened to his position as our vassal. He will continue to be useful to us in our future efforts." Despite his paralysis, she felt an imperceptible tightening of Pierre's demeanor. This could go either way. She made herself wait. If she presented as too eager, she could condemn Danny Mac to death.

"Is this a desire of your heart, my lady?" he asked softly.

Again, she felt Danny Mac's life hanging on her answer. "He has proved useful. I believe we can use him to bring our other enemies who tried to destroy us."

Pierre looked at her for several seconds. Then he smiled with delight. "If he brings them to us, he shall live. If he fails, you will kill him yourself."

As much as it cost her, she replied, "As you wish."

Pierre barked to the men flanking the door. "Take him away and lock him in. I will call for him later."

Kenann forced herself not to even glance in Danny Mac's direction. She sent up her own silent plea to her heavenly Father for strength and courage.

37

NITA AND PINKY asked Mrs. Gage to gather the troops. When all were assembled, Nita took command. "Pinky and I have discussed it and feel the damsel-in-distress routine is our best option."

Mrs. Gage nodded and appeared to be considering this tact. She obviously was familiar with past operations using this method. Mrs. Gage enlightened the rest of the group. "The women will park their car in walking distance of the castle and disable the vehicle either with sugar in the tank or pulling apart one of the hoses. But it has to be something not easily fixed. They show up on the doorstep as the quintessential damsels in distress. Once inside, they will make themselves hard to get rid of. They tag team into distraction and annoyance. While one person is dealing with one of them, the other goes off in another direction until they feel like they are herding cats."

Nita smiled. "Very well-depicted, Gabby girl."

Carter queried, "What is our role?"

Nita turned to him. "We will go in wired so you will hear what is going on and can direct us as needed from here."

"What if they catch the wire?" Carter asked.

Pinky grinned. "Then we shall count on the cavalry to come riding in."

He countered, "Why don't we just use the cavalry first."

"Where is the fun in that? Come now, Mr. Carter. Let us do what we do best." Nita gave him her most sultry smile.

He answered, "Whatever." But he couldn't help but soften it with a grin.

Mrs. Gage took note of this thawing of Carters attitude and planned to use Nita if any further influence was needed.

Jake interjected, "I'd like to do some aerial reconnaissance."

Andy laughed, "You just want to go up in the chopper."

"Well, yeah!" Jake emphasized his words with laughter.

Mrs. Gage added, "We do need to see what our options are for invasion." Jake again marveled at her resemblance to a military commander. She continued, "There will be room for three plus the pilot. Mr. Carter, I suggest you, Jacob, and myself."

"Agreed. Can we go now?"

"The staff is standing by on a word from us."

Jake stood. "Let's do this!"

Andy asked, "What do you want us to do, sir?" Carter stamped down on his annoyance that Andy directed this question at Jake.

"Can you set the ladies up with the comm devices? Also, create a mobile base station in case we decide to move in closer?"

"You got it, boss." Judy nudged him.

He looked at her; she turned to Carter. Andy cringed inwardly. *Crap!*

Kenann continued to stand beside Pierre's chair with her hand on his shoulder. It made her skin crawl.

"Have you truly come back to me, Inanna?"

"Yes, Pierre."

"You are lying."

Her heart lurched. She continued the bluff. "I am not, Pierre. And I do not appreciate your attitude. You would do well to respect who stands beside you." The silence was unbearable. She continued to stare straight ahead and willed her hands to remain steady.

He finally spoke, "I had to be sure, Your Highness."

"Do not ever question me again, Pierre." He did not respond. She prayed he was sufficiently moved to caution. She knew her position was tenuous at best.

He continued as if their exchange had not occurred. "If you will look at the monitors, you will see the locations and level of flow through various pipelines positioned throughout the world." He turned his gaze up to her to inquire if she could see what he indicated.

"Yes, I see, Pierre. And these pipelines all belong to *our* people?"

"All of them. They belong to me—and to you."

She took note of his proprietary attitude. She wished she had made connections to others in this crazy group. She would have exploited this to undermine his power. She began plotting how she might get him to introduce her to others in the upper echelon. "What are your plans, Pierre?"

"Many years before I was born, this plan was implemented. It has taken seventy years to develop the infrastructure in secret. We are nearing completion of the final phases."

"Explain."

"We have created our own secret pipelines that intersect with all major pipelines in the world. We have installed valves that are controlled by us electronically. That is what you are looking at now. We keep them open slightly and siphon off minuscule amounts of crude from each line for our own profit."

"What is the endgame?" Even though she knew, she needed some time to absorb the gravity at what was being presented. She had discovered the bones of the plan on her last nightly sojourn, prompting her resurrection as Inanna.

"When we are ready, we shut off the valves that lie past ours, and we take over the oil supply of every oil field in the world. We also have plans to take control of the fields themselves. We are using ISIS, who is embedded throughout the world to provide guerilla warfare assistance. They can take all the credit they want. Our people who are positioned for this event will be the ones in control. By the time anyone tracks our valves and has any ability to stop it, we will have successfully crippled the world economy and we will be in charge."

Even though she felt her voice constricting, she verbally applauded the plan. These people were more dangerous than she had ever believed. Since he was fresh off his pleasure at revealing his plan, she decided to check out what he was thinking about Danny Mac.

"Will you be sending Daniel to bring the others?"

"Is that your desire?"

"As long as they are out there, our efforts will be at risk. They know too much." Again, she prayed for the Holy Spirit to guide her.

"That is my thinking exactly. Do you think he can bring them here?"

"Daniel will be able to do it. They listen to him."

"And then it will be your pleasure to destroy them. That will cement your position."

Kenann adopted her most imperious persona and spoke quietly but with command, "Do I need to *cement* my position, Pierre?"

"You misunderstand. I believe in you completely. I am the one who recognized you. But we need to introduce you to the rest of the ruling council."

"Weren't they present in Egypt?"

"Yes, but as you know, things deteriorated. It will take some good will to achieve their trust again. I know you for who you are. They will need to be convinced."

"I see. Well, let us waste no time then. I need to reveal myself completely to the others. I have finally shed my earthly persona of Kenann. Her complete madness enabled me to emerge fully and finally. Convene the ruling council, Pierre."

The other men in the room began to question if this woman truly was the reincarnated goddess, Inanna.

38

Although Danny Mac and Kenann are in different parts of the castle, both heard the commotion being created in the front hall at the main entrance.

Kenann told Pierre she would deal with the intrusion. He agreed. Kenann walked slowly and with regality along the hallway until she came to the balcony overlooking the hall. She did not recognize the women who were creating havoc below; but something told her that this had Mrs. Gage written all over it, and she rejoiced.

She called out as imperiously as possible. Her voice echoed off the stone walls. "Bring them to me."

These men had not been privy to the exchange between Pierre and her earlier; but they responded to her commanding voice and presence and complied. The women smiled and looked in awe at the paintings and tapestries hanging from the massive walls as they ascended the stairs. The men flanked the women closely. Considering the chaos they incited in a very short time, they did not want to let them loose again. When they reached the place that Kenann stood, the men appeared to wait for orders.

Pinky jumped in quickly. "Pardon our intrusion, Ma'am. Our car broke down, and we are simply helpless with anything mechanic." Pinky laughed to herself. Nita could take apart and put together an engine faster than anyone she knew.

Nita added, "We hate to bother you. Would you be able to spare these strapping young men to…take care of us?" She gave the one closest to her a look that left little to the imagination. Pinky giggled vacuously.

"Certainly, but first, you must warm yourself by our fire and have some tea." She turned her attention to the men. "Tell Pierre I have the situation well in hand and will join him shortly."

The taller of the two men answered, "Yes, Ma'am."

Kenann turned her attention back to the ladies. "Come with me please." She led them in the direction of the room she shared with Danny Mac. Once there, the guard in the hallway hesitated to let her in, confused by the presence of these two women. Kenann spoke quietly but firmly, "These women have had car trouble. We need to entertain them before sending them on their way. We must not appear churlish. Pierre has asked me to handle this. Do you understand?"

"Yes, Ma'am."

"If you would be so kind to await my orders." She turned the key in the lock and entered the room. Danny Mac jumped from the armchair by the window when he saw her. He raised an eyebrow at the other women. Kenann quickly took charge. She was balancing her charade of Inanna to any listening ears with wanting to communicate with Danny Mac and possibly these emissaries of Mrs. Gage. "Daniel, these ladies have had some misfortune with their vehicle and appeared on our doorstep. I thought it would be nice if we offered them tea before we gave them assistance."

"Certainly. Let me pull up some chairs around the fire."

Kenann went to the door to ask the man to bring a tea service and was shaken to see Pierre coming down the hall toward them. She stepped out, closing the door behind her.

"What are you doing?" Pierre hissed.

"Pierre, these ladies were wreaking havoc downstairs. I had to gain control of the situation and fast. I brought them to the room I have occupied with Danny Mac because that is the only room I knew. I did not want to welcome them into a room with dust covers on the furniture. How would that look? We need to find out what they are about. They could be spies."

"I would have thought you knew every inch of this place by the way you wandered its halls day and night."

Kenann thought quickly, "What are you talking about? If you are referring to the activities of Kenann, I have no recollection of her madness."

This seemed to appease him. "Very well but, find out what they are about quickly and get rid of them."

"With pleasure." She allowed herself to give him an unholy smile. His attempt at a return smile was gruesome. She had to control the shudder that threatened to overtake her.

She turned to the man at the door and asked him to bring them a tea cart and nodded to Pierre as she reentered the suite of rooms.

"Excuse my delay. Good help is so hard to find."

Pinky continued her role. "Ain't that the truth. This is some pile you have here, Ma'am. Do you own it?

Nita feigned shock. "Pinky! That is not polite."

Kenann interjected, "Think nothing of it. Yes, it is owned by my consort, Pierre."

Pinky continued, "Oooh, *consort*! Sounds fancy."

"Pinky!" Nita warned.

Kenann laughed. Danny Mac just sat back and waited to see what was up her sleeve. The tea cart arrived, and Kenann continued as she poured each a cup from the china pot. "What brings you ladies to this area?"

"Oh, we are on vacation." Pinky softly tapped out *gage* in Morse code with her teaspoon.

It took a couple of times for it to register with Danny Mac. When it did, he forced himself not to overreact. He looked at Kenann and gave her the prearranged hand signal for yes. Kenann did not question how he knew. She simply trusted him.

Kenann smiled broadly. "That is wonderful!." She couldn't help sighing happily. They all smiled in return. Pierre puzzled at this from his monitor screen but reasoned that Inanna had just thought of a plan. "Well, what are your plans while you are here?"

Nita took over. "We are checking out the area for a friend. She wants to bring her very large family here but did not know if there was enough to do. She wanted to find out how many people there actually were. She hates crowds."

Kenann understood. "Oh, what you see is what you get. There may be a few people tucked away but not enough to give her any problems, I would imagine."

"Wonderful. Do you live here or are you vacationing too?"

"Visiting, actually. Daniel will be taking a trip soon to gather some friends of ours." She gave Danny Mac a telling look. Pierre interpreted this as a message between Inanna and her vassal.

A thought struck Nita, and she turned up the sultry charm. "Say, how about you come with me?" She reached over and laid her hand lightly over his. "You can give me a ride back into town and then show me the sights before you take off on your little trip. What do you say?" Her mouth was a perfect pout.

Danny Mac turned to both Kenann and Inanna for direction.

She pondered as both. "Let's not be hasty. We have not finalized your plans yet, Daniel."

He replied with, "As you wish." Both were reminded of her favorite movie, *Princess Bride*. She smiled at him.

Pinky had an idea of her own and squealed for effect. "Oooh! Can we stay here for the night? I've never slept in a castle before. Oh please, oh please! I promise we won't be any bother. You and this young man can figure out your plans, and we can be off tomorrow. Oh, please, oh please!"

Nita purred, "That would be delightful!" She gave Danny Mac a come-hither look.

Kenann wanted to tell her not to push her luck but restrained herself. This was business. She sighed indulgently and said, "Let me confer with Pierre, and I will let you know. If you will excuse me."

Nita's smile appeared catlike. "Take your time, dear."

Kenann raised an eyebrow. She was ready to pounce when Danny Mac spoke. "Pierre will have specific orders for my journey. I will await them."

She came back to her role and rose. "I will not be long." She did not look at Nita but hoped she got the message. Life-and-death role-playing was one thing, but messing with Danny Mac was another.

As soon as Kenann had left the room, Nita made a pretense of fluffing her luxurious hair and pulled the ear wig from its place. She took a tube of lip stick from her bag and expertly placed the comm device in her mouth as she applied the bold lipstick. This was going to be fun. She walked slowly toward Danny Mac, whose eyes flared as he recognized her intent.

He stood up and started to back away when she pinned him against the side table. She slid into him and brought her lips to his. They were a match in height. She enjoyed the play of her tongue on his as she transferred the comm device. Once he felt the metal, he relaxed knowing what she was about. He would never admit, even to himself, how skillful Nita's seductive powers were.

39

INANNA RETURNED FROM a lengthy conference with Pierre, he noticed the smear of lipstick on Danny Mac's lips. She raised an eyebrow and her look was feral.

He tried to utilize their previous hand signals; but she ignored him. He looked for any sign of Kenann.

"All right, ladies. Pierre has consented to you being our guest tonight. Daniel will leave with you tomorrow. But he will have his duties, Nita. I'm afraid he will not be able to *show you around.*" Her smile was ice-cold. "I will show you to your rooms so you may freshen up."

Pinky sensed the tension and offered sweetly, "That would be lovely. Thank you, Ma'am. I just realized I don't even know your name."

Kenann gave her a very direct gaze, steeling her voice, she said, "Inanna."

Danny Mac prayed to God Kenann was still in there.

Carter looked at Mrs. Gage. "Nita is playing a dangerous game, Gabrielle."

Mrs. Gage could not disagree but decided to change the subject nonetheless. "What is our plan, John?"

"Let's wait to see what Kenann and Danny can reveal through the wire."

They did not have long to wait. Kenann came back into the room, and if she shut the door a little harder than necessary, no one acknowledged it.

Danny Mac spoke first. "These women could be a nuisance, Inanna. Why did you let them stay?"

Kenann gave him a feral smile, which did nothing to reassure him. "Oh, a cat likes to play with her prey before she goes in for the kill, don't you know?"

He cleared his throat. While Kenann took Nita and Pinky away, he had gone to the bathroom and placed the comm device deep in his ear. "What do you and Pierre desire of me?" Danny Mac attempted to focus Kenann on their task at hand.

Kenann appeared to shake off confusing thoughts and looked at him. "You are to bring our enemies here so we can dispatch them."

She said it with such conviction, Danny Mac feared Pierre had implemented further hypnotic control over Kenann. It was a fear shared by those who were listening a few short miles away. "What am I to say?"

Kenann sighed in exasperation. "Do I have to do all your thinking, Daniel? Tell them you escaped. Bring them here to *rescue* me." Her laugh chilled Danny Mac to the bone. Jake and Mrs. Gage looked at each other; their hearts sinking. Kenann continued, "And you must produce Blade as well."

Danny Mac's head whipped around. "What?"

"You heard me. We want everyone who was in Egypt *here*. Do not oppose me on this, Daniel."

Danny Mac knew he was being watched closely on the monitor. His role-playing was being scrutinized as closely as Kenann's. "Yes, milady!" He bowed his head slightly to acknowledge.

Across the valley, Mrs. Gage straightened from her close monitoring of the voice transmission. "Time for a counsel of war." Danny Mac heard and concurred.

40

THEY SAT AROUND the table, communicating with Nita and Pinky with their remaining comm device. They had gone out on the balcony under the guise of checking out the view, hoping any surveillance equipment would not pick up on their conversation. They kept their comments cryptic, nevertheless. Danny Mac took their cue and walked out on his balcony as well to listen. He was pleased but not surprised to learn they were ensconced on the next mountain.

"That Inanna is some kind of chick." Pinky heard Mrs. Gage explain that Pierre had hypnotized Kenann at one point, and they feared he had regained at least partial control of her. She also cautioned Nita to cease and desist her seduction of Danny Mac. Kenann's control was tenuous.

Pinky related this to Nita. "You better quit hitting on that guy, Nita. That chick looks like she could do you in." She added because she felt it, "This is already a spooky place, Nita. I don't want to have to keep one eye open all night."

Nita pouted. "All right. I hear you loud and clear."

They both sat quietly, looking out over the valley while the council of war proceeded.

Carter had the floor. "I could see how this could work to our advantage…or go completely south."

"Exactly!" Andy agreed. He was more worried than he ever been about the outcome of this operation.

Granny spoke, "Get me in there."

Everyone turned to look at her. She sat looking straight ahead and repeated. "Get me in there. She is my granddaughter. I can reach her even if she is under Pierre's power."

Judy spoke softly, "Granny, if Danny Mac can't do it, how do you know you can."

Granny turned to look her. "I know. Danny Mac, can you hear me?"

He coughed in reply.

"Get me in there."

He leaned on the rail and cupped his chin in both hands in apparent contemplation. He whispered, "Moira."

"You heard me."

He spoke as if only the two of them could hear. "I'm afraid it may have gone too far, Moira. I'm scared."

"Now you listen to me, young man. You are a warrior of God. You will not lose heart. Do you understand me?"

He whispered huskily, "Yes, Ma'am."

"Now get me in there."

He grinned despite himself. "Yes, Ma'am."

He knew he would not be able to go to Pierre and Kenann unannounced or unbidden so he waited. When she came to get him for dinner, he asked her conversationally, "Perhaps I can get my phone Pierre confiscated and begin contacting the others to lay the groundwork for our plan."

She turned and looked at him. He searched her eyes. She gave him an enigmatic smile and said, "All right." Her look was predatory. She came to him and stood within an inch of him. "Pierre says I can have anything my heart desires." She began tracing her finger over Danny's chest. She looked up into his eyes and said, "I think my heart desires you." She turned and walked slowly to the door. She tossed a look over her shoulder. "Now come eat dinner, Daniel, and I will give you dessert later."

Nita and Pinky were not prepared when Pierre rolled into the dining room in his chair and breathing apparatus attached to his chair. Pinky swallowed audibly. Nita took her hand under the table and squeezed. Danny Mac stood and helped position him at the table.

Pierre hissed, "Don't touch me!"

Kenann cajoled, "Oh, Pierre! Don't hold a grudge." He looked at her for several seconds.

Pinky could not stand the tension a moment longer. "Thank you so much for letting us stay tonight. I can't wait to get home and tell my folks that I actually stayed the night in a castle. This is really awesome. I can't imagine living in a castle. I live in an apartment."

Nita laughed to herself. *Liar! You live in a castle too.*

Everyone settled into their dinner while Pinky prattled on. Pierre sat at the head of the table, watching the others eat. He had survived via a feeding tube since he awoke in a backroom surgical unit operated by the order. He hated it, and he hated the man who put him in that chair. One way or another, he was going to die a slow and torturously painful death.

The meal was obviously uncomfortable for everyone, except Inanna who carried the conversation after Pinky ran out of steam. "I've laid out some night things for you ladies. And I've asked the men to bring in plenty of wood to keep the fire going tonight. Don't want the light to go out. You never know what might be lurking in the shadows."

Her laughter appeared harmless enough, Nita thought, *so why is the hair standing up on the back of my neck?*

"First thing in the morning, Daniel will take you to the village." *That's better,* Pinky thought. *I cannot wait to get out of this stupid place.* "Pierre, Daniel is in need of his phone to contact our…*friends.*" Nita and Pinky looked at Danny Mac. *This was not good. Not good at all.*

"I will ensure it is taken to his room along with my instructions. Is that clear?" He turned his gaze to Danny Mac who nodded.

"Thank you, Pierre. We will meet with you in the morning before Daniel and the ladies depart." She turned her gaze to Nita and Pinky. "Now, if you will allow me to escort you to your room, I think we should all turn in."

They had no real choice but to stand and be led from the room.

Danny Mac asked Pierre, "What are my instructions?"

"You will be told when I choose, not before. Now leave me in peace."

When Danny Mac did not move, one of Pierre's men stood up. Danny Mac stood and faced the man, daring him to make a move. He was itching to vent his spleen on someone; this was as good a time as any. The man lunged. Swift as a snake, Danny Mac struck. First to the soft part of the man's neck with a crushing blow to his vocal cord, finishing him off with an elbow strike to the back of his head. He went down like a tree. Danny Mac didn't look back. He simply walked out and mounted the steps to his room. He slammed the door open and paced. He was like a pent-up tiger warring with himself. He did not know what kind of man he was. He was sick to death of living under the shadow of his past and now this crazy society he was fighting. Kenann was possibly lost to him. God seemed far away. He charged out on the balcony, taking in great gulps of the cold air.

He sensed rather than heard Kenann come in and close the door. She looked him in the eye as he turned then she went to a picture on the wall and unplugged the accent light above it. He realized it held the surveillance camera for this room. She turned back and began unbuttoning her dress. She stopped long enough to toss the key that locked them in to the side table.

"Kenann?"

"Inanna," she answered.

"No, you are Kenann. I am your husband. I have spoken to Granny."

At this, Kenann paused and looked quizzical as if fighting with a distant memory. She shook it off and continued disrobing. Danny Mac took the comm device and folded it deeply into the chair cushion on the balcony. He closed the door behind him as he reentered the room. If he was going to make love to Inanna, he did not want any witnesses.

Granny slipped from the group. Going to her room, she dropped to her knees. "Oh Lord, we need you. Danny and Kenann are under attack by the evil one. Please, oh Lord! Rescue them. Be their strength and guide. They need your mighty power. Right now, oh Lord!" She bent forward, groaning inwardly knowing the Holy Spirit would interpret the desires of her heart to the Father. When she pulled her old bones up from the floor several hours later, she knew she had prayed through.

Nita and Pinky were in conference with Mrs. Gage from their balcony. If anyone was observing, it appeared they were only talking to themselves. The conversation was somber. Things had taken a bad turn. Pinky was spooked and had placed a straight-backed chair under the doorknob. Mrs. Gage allowed herself a smile. All they could do at this point was wait till morning and see if they truly were able to leave with Danny Mac as promised. If they were detained and things got dicey, they would move in.

Carter weighed in on this. "We cannot afford to lose that data on those pipelines. If we move in like gangbusters, they will crash and burn it."

"I will not put any of these people in jeopardy." Mrs. Gage squared off with him.

"You knew going in that we weren't playing. Don't make me pull rank."

Mrs. Gage did not blink. She stared him down and plotted.

Danny Mac had found another way to vent his spleen. Kenann's aggression with him did little to remind him he was no longer that man. They were brutal with each other in a way they never would have been before. Both were set on conquest in an unholy battle. Granny was waging her own war for them.

Dawn broke. Danny Mac turned to a sleeping Kenann, feeling shame at the way he had treated her throughout the hours of the night. He turned on his back and stared at the ceiling. *How could this have gone so wrong? God, please help me.*

Kenann stirred and turned to him sleepily. She snuggled in and murmured, "Good morning, sweetheart."

Danny Mac started, "Kenann?"

She continued to snuggle. "Hmmm?"

"Is it you?"

She looked up then. "Who else would it be, silly?"

He pulled her to him in relief. "I think I'm going mad."

She looked around at that point. Memories began flooding back. "Danny?" She waited till he was looking at her. "What is going on?"

"I think Pierre has been exercising some form of mind control. What happened when you went back to his room that last time?"

"I don't know. We talked about how he wanted everyone here like he said before."

"Did he do anything differently? Did you hear anything?"

She pondered carefully. She knew it was important. "I heard a clock chime. Well, it was more like the sound of a hammer hitting a gong."

As soon as she said it, she knew. Danny Mac realized it at the same time. On the platform in Egypt, she had gone off-script right after the gong had sounded. He must have used this sound in her apartment in Memphis as well.

"Oh, Danny Mac! What can we do?"

"Well, I don't know, but I know who does."

And with that, he enclosed her hands in his and prayed. "Father, you are master of all things. We praise and honor you for your sovereign power. We call on that power to intercede now with Kenann. Do not allow Pierre to exert control over her mind in any way. From this moment forth, when she hears the sound of the gong that has been used to control her, it will now remind her of your love and influence in her life and she will be infused with power from on high. Thank you, Lord Jesus. And it is through the power of your name that we ask and believe these things."

They were both still for several seconds. When Kenann opened her eyes and looked at Danny Mac, her eyes shown with hope and confidence. "Okay, let's do this, partner."

Danny took another moment to repent his lack of faith and say a private thank you for God's grace in his own life, asking for strength to honor Him in all he does.

41

Danny Mac and Kenann entered Pierre's command center together. He turned his chair to face them and waited. Kenann came to stand beside him, placing a proprietary hand on his shoulder. "It is time to begin, Daniel. I hope you understand what is at stake. Pierre has decided all of our enemies must be brought here. If you fail, you will fail me. Do you understand?"

"Yes, milady," nodding his head.

She reached behind her. "Here is your phone so you can begin making contact. Now go and take those dreadful women with you." She had steeled herself for this moment as he turned and walked away, leaving her with Pierre. Their earlier words of goodbye would have to sustain her through what lay ahead.

Danny Mac went to the women's room and knocked. Nita answered. He inquired, "Are you ready to leave?"

Pinky called from inside the room, "I'll say we *are*!"

He led them down the stairs and took the keys offered by the man at the door. Nita once again looked for the boy Vincenzo had described as his son. She had seen no one fitting his description. She promised herself to not leave this village until she knew what had happened to him. Danny Mac shook his head, tapping his ear when Pinky started to talk freely. She understood. They parked the car in the village and going to the nearest coffee shop called Carter.

"We're out. Come get us," giving him the name and directions to the shop.

Danny Mac was embraced all round. Granny held back. Danny Mac wrapped her in his arms and clung to her, knowing instinctively she had fought for him in prayer. She patted his back in comfort and love. He smiled despite his concern for Kenann. They gathered in the library for their council of war.

Carter wasted no time before barking, "Report, MacKenzie!"

Danny Mac checked in with Kenann on the comm device he left in her care. "Can you hear me, Kenann?" She responded with a cough. He continued as he addressed the group.

"As you know, the order has an intricate complex of pipelines throughout the world. If they actually pull it off, they really might have a shot at controlling the global economy. We have to get our hands on that grid data. And we need to be introduced to the rest of the ruling council. This is a personal vendetta by Pierre against us. The other power brokers are too busy holding the order together or covering their own tracks. We have to find a way to flush them out."

Judy asked, "Are we really bringing Blade here?"

Jake answered, "Not unless we absolutely have to."

Danny Mac sighed. "Unfortunately, we may not be able to complete our efforts without him. Here is my plan."

They talked for the better part of that day. At one point, Mrs. Gage gained Carter's attention and indicated she wished a private word.

"Do you think Whittaker is strong enough to accompany Blade?"

"Yes, I believe so. I will call him and give him his orders."

"First, let me talk to Mr. Baer so he can make arrangements for me to speak privately to Blade. God help me for doing this to his dear mother."

"God help us all." Mrs. Gage stared at Carter as he turned and walked away.

"I'm coming with him!" CJ demanded.

"Mr. Baer, that is beyond your responsibilities."

"Bulls——t! That kid *is* my responsibility. If he goes, I go."

"As you wish, Mr. Baer. Ask Whittaker to make your arrangements and bring Blade to a private place so we may talk."

Blade was beyond excited about the prospect of joining the others in their mission. He told her he had the perfect cover story for his mother. Mrs. Gage had no doubt. It took two days but they were all finally assembled together at the chateau and ready for the next phase. Nerves ran high. Blade was beside himself with joy. Danny Mac had been in contact with Pierre and bragged at how easily he had gathered all the players. Pierre railed at him when he did not produce Carter. Danny Mac was ready.

"If I brought Carter, I would have risked the National Security Council coming down on us. He was not in Egypt and therefore not part of this original group." Pierre was only slightly mollified.

Kenann/Inanna had completed her part of the plan by convincing Pierre that he needed to assemble the ruling council to witness his triumph over his enemies. They wasted no time responding to his summons. Kenann had forgone the bedsheet for this occasion and had been able to find an appropriately elegant black dress to greet the men and women as they arrived. Kenann had also been busy in her efforts to make subtle alliances with the men. She had asked God to show her who she would be able to convince and trust when the time came. She only found one, completely unaware it was Vincenzo's son. He had realized soon after coming to Istanbul with Pierre that he was a madman. He saw no way out at that point considering the threats they all received regarding assassinating their loved ones should they consider betrayal. Kenann did not reveal herself or their plan to Paulo; she simply insinuated she was concerned about Pierre's stability and may need his support at some point. He had agreed. He figured this lady was at least more stable than Pierre. She might be one step closer to getting out of this mess.

Mrs. Gage looked at each face in the semicircle around her. Danny Mac, Moira, Jacob, little Blade with his expectant face, Andrew and Judy, and even Angelo who risked swift retribution for his betrayal. They were all ready to do battle together again. She couldn't be more proud. Carter and CJ stood with Whittaker and Johnson on the stairs a few paces above them.

Carter looked like a general addressing his troops. "Ladies and gentlemen, this is it. We have one shot. Let's make it count."

The group shared a collective grin and nodded as one. Blade figured it was the closest he was going to get to a huddle roar and went with it. They were able to fit into one oversized utility vehicle. Danny Mac drove. "Kenann, we are on our way. Have you made preparations in the armory?"

She murmured softly, "Umm hmm"

"Good. Tell Pierre to assemble the council. I will escort in my quarry."

Kenann entered the room, which looked like a simple cocktail party. Obviously powerful, wealthy people from all over the world were assembled in this one room. She recognized none of their faces but realized these were the people who were the real power brokers. Even if world leaders were unaware, these were the people who shaped and molded international policies behind the scenes. She took her place beside Pierre and assumed the now familiar hand on his shoulder. She bent and whispered, "Daniel is almost here with his package."

Pierre's eyes took on a sinister gleam. He raised his voice. "Ladies and gentlemen, may I have your attention? Please follow me to our front hall." He turned his chair and led the way. In the center of the large main hall, he had ordered an elevated platform be constructed. He wanted the advantage of height to compensate for his status at chair level. He would dominate.

Kenann joined him on the platform, flanked by the council as Danny Mac and the rest walked in as one. Pierre's security detail moved the group *en masse* as instructed to just inside the wide doorway of a side room adjacent to the foyer. "So glad of you to join us." Danny Mac started to step forward but was hindered at gunpoint. Kenann held her breath. *This was not good.*

"Darling, Inanna. You were so wise to call for the council to witness the demise of this despicable group of vermin." At that, a large iron gate dropped in front of their faces.

Kenann tried to hold her voice steady. "Pierre, Daniel has been a faithful servant to us."

"No!" he screamed. "He will die with the others."

She made herself touch his shoulder. He jerked his chair away from her touch and came down the ramp to confront his prey. Kenann looked her loved ones in the eye and felt completely helpless. She took a deep breath and squared her shoulders. "Pierre, stop!"

He whirled around. "You *dare* challenge me?"

She changed tact. "Remember, we have a presentation for our guests here. I know your zeal regarding these people, but let us focus our attention on our distinguished guests." She waved a presenting arm in a semicircle toward the council members standing below her.

He looked up at her and seemed to regain his composure. "Of course. Thank you, Inanna. I must remember my priorities." He turned to his security and ordered the prisoners be taken to the secure room off the command center. He wanted them to know what he had accomplished and what they were powerless to prevent. He addressed the crowd. "I apologize for my momentary digression. If you will accompany me, I will show you what all our efforts have accomplished. We are ready to take the next step in this millennia's world domination." Pierre went to his private elevator while the smartly clad group mounted the stairs to the command center on the second level.

She stole a glance at Danny Mac as she passed. She raised an eyebrow. He answered yes with an imperceptible nod. *Showtime.*

42

NITA PULLED HERSELF over the parapet of Danny Mac's balcony. She had started in the wee hours of the morning at the base of the cliff. During their aerial reconnaissance Jake observed this potential infiltration point. She pulled off her stocking cap, released her long red hair, and allowed herself a moment to take a long draft from her water bottle. She clipped it back on to her belt and checked her weapon. She spoke to those listening, "I'm in."

Danny Mac turned to the others as if talking to them. "By my count, most of the men are here in the command center guarding the council. There are three unaccounted for. Watch your back."

"Roger that," Carter responded. "We wait your go, Red."

"In due time, love. In due time." Her Irish brogue had thickened with the adrenaline of the moment. She had found Danny's balcony by the white cloth tied to the rail. The back face of the castle was endless rows of rooms with small balconies. Had it not been for that marker, she would have wasted precious time getting her bearings to the armory. She knew she had to scale four balconies to get to her desired destination. This was as dangerous as the long climb up the cliff face. It was a matter of timing. She stood on the edge of the rail with her hand against the stone wall of the castle. She bounced on the balls of her feet and found her rhythm.

One, two, three...leap. She rolled to a stop. *Up again. Balance, breathe. One, two, three...leap. So far, so good.* Again, she counted and jumped. Just as she pushed off, her foot lost its purchase, throwing her off balance. She strained for flight and flung her hands out for anything solid. One hand grasped a single ledge stone. Her fingers strained to hold the weight of her body as she swayed over a thousand-foot precipice. She felt the sweat pouring into her eyes and willed herself to calm. She found her rhythm again and strained up with her other hand to grab a spindle, eventually pulling herself up and over the railing. She did not wait or think long enough to lose her nerve but went straight to the final rail. *Up, balance, count, and leap. Solid ground. Now let's shut these freaks down and go home.*

Kenann positioned herself so she could see into the glass-enclosed observation room and the faces of her friends and loved ones. *Almost there, almost there.* She took a gamble and edged over to Paulo. "I need you to trust me, Paulo," she whispered to him.

"Yes, what is it you wish of me?"

"I need you to unlock the door on our captives." He jerked his head to face her. She added quickly, "Don't react. Just listen to me. Pierre is insane. He must be stopped. Those ladies who came here a few days ago were sent to find you by your father, Vincenzo."

He did turn; but slowly this time to look at her again for confirmation. Her eyes confirmed she was telling him the truth. He wanted so much to see his family again. He would do whatever it took. "I will do it."

"Good man. Be careful."

He started to move, but she put a restraining hand on his arm. "We need to be very casual. If you leave my side so soon after we have spoken, you will draw attention to yourself. Now laugh at what I have just said." He hesitated only a moment and then threw back his head and laughed. He shook his head and grinned. She did the same.

Pierre called out, "Are you fraternizing with the help, my dear?" There was an edge to his voice.

"Just sharing what I plan to do to our captives. He approves." This seemed to appease him. She waived Paulo away with a laugh.

Luckily, he understood the gravity of his mission and his need for caution. He did not go directly to the glass enclosure, but joined some other guards by the window. He remained casual.

Nita had donned her favorite travel pantsuit made of black spandex blend. She loved it for its durability and wrinkle-free properties. It looked great for a casual date or a night full of ass-kicking. She stepped out into the hallway and approached the man monitoring the hallway below. He turned and gave her a quizzical expression. He had seen this lady here earlier. He thought she left. Was she part of the council? Nita turned on her catlike charm. With a soft purring sound, she trailed her hand up his chest and over his shoulder as she made to move behind him. He was silenced and laid quietly on the floor within seconds. She moved languidly down the steps as if she had nothing better to do in case she was observed. She made for the front door when a very large man appeared from the shadows.

"What are you doing? Who let you in here?"

"I was invited, big boy. And I was just going for some fresh air. These castles can be horribly stuffy." He looked up and realized his partner was not at his post and gave a low rumble in his chest. *Here we go*, she thought.

He lunged for her. In one swift motion, she leapt against the wall, propelling herself onto his back. Pulling off her scarf, she had him incapacitated in short order. She fell back, his limp form pinning her to the floor. She rolled his weight off her and ran to the main door. "Welcome, friends."

Carter, Whittaker, Johnson, and Pinky ran in, carrying weapons. They swiftly made their way back to the armory and gathered additional firepower for their friends.

Carter whispered, "We're on our way."

Nita added, "One still unaccounted for, so stay sharp."

In their earbuds, Pierre's mechanical voice cracked, "Oh, please, do come join our party."

They froze in their tracks. Carter nodded to go into the closest room, out of the direct line of fire of the hallway.

"What do you want, Pierre?"

"Oh, many things, many things. Is this Mr. Carter?"

"Go to hell!"

Things were heating up quickly. Inside the command center, it appeared all bets were off. Pierre had Blade on the floor at his feet, claiming him as the long-overdue sacrifice. The ruling council members were looking dubious as they congregated together out of the way of the melee.

Before Paulo could make good on his promise, one of the other guards had taken it upon himself to do a search of the captives and found Danny Mac's earbud. He put a gun to his head to ensure silence as he removed and took it to Pierre. Pierre had then ordered them out of the glass-enclosed room and on their knees in execution position.

He called to Kenann. "Inanna, to take your rightful place, you must come and complete the sacrifice of blood. Take this knife from my hand and *do it*."

"Pierre, please! You must stop."

"I said, DO IT!"

When she hesitated, he nodded to one of his men, who struck the small gong that was sitting on the floor under one of the tables. Kenann froze. Her eyes took on a glassy appearance. Danny Mac looked up and willed her back to him. She put her hands to her head and whirled around, bending over at the waist as if in pain. Pierre's smile revealed his enjoyment in the suffering his mind control was causing her. Kenann raised herself up slowly to her full height and turned to look at Pierre. She smiled. Then raised her arm and put a bullet between his eyes.

43

EVERYTHING HAPPENED AT once. Blade rolled into the man to his left, clipping him at the knees and sending him flying backwards. Kenann grabbed his weapon in midair and knocked him unconscious with it before he hit the ground. Danny Mac and Andy made short work of the two guards behind them, turning their weapons on the remaining guards. One of them was Paulo, who took the opportunity to knock out the man to his right.

Kenann put her pistol to the temple of the man to his left and whispered, "Don't even think about it."

Angelo had tried to shield Granny and Judy with his body but soon found they had other ideas. They scrambled to their feet, grabbing any discarded weapon they could find and went after the council. Angelo had no choice but try to keep up. Some of the ruling council had already made it to the door before Granny and Judy could corral them. They were met by Carter and his crew running up the hallway toward them. They waved them back into the room and turned them over to Granny and Judy who had things well in hand. Angelo stood by, looking a little stunned. All the guards were subdued by that time, and the victors were beginning to relax.

Out of the corner of her eye, Kenann saw the one remaining guard fill the doorway to the room and raise his machine gun to fire. She turned sideways and dropped him with her handgun.

Danny Mac caught her eye from across the room and grinned. "Good shootin', Tex."

44

AFTER A THOROUGH search, the ruling council and captured guards were herded into the glass enclosure until they could determine the next course of action.

Carter's eyes roamed the group. "Everyone okay?"

Each person inspected the person beside them until it was determined that no one had been injured.

Danny Mac had Kenann wrapped in his arms. "Kenann's idea to disable the guard's weapons prior to our arrival was a good one." Granny made her way across the room and was enveloped by Danny Mac and Kenann. Danny Mac whispered, "Thank you!"

Granny smiled. "Once in a while, you have to do your fighting on your knees."

Kenann looked at them quizzically; but they only smiled at each other.

Nita and Pinky had Paulo cornered. Pinky was shaking her finger under his nose, undoubtedly lecturing him about bringing grief to his family. Head hanging low, he looked appropriately chagrined.

Andy, Jake, and Carter were scouring over the technical equipment. Andy was copying evidence into flash drives as fast as his fingers could move in the event someone had activated a kill switch.

Judy stood with Angelo. "You doing okay, big guy?"

"I cannot fathom the way all of you worked to control this room. Except for a few, you are not professionals."

Judy grinned like a mischievous child. "We're pretty cool, aren't we?" And feeling playful, she showed him exploding fingers. "*BA-BAM!*"

Blade was sitting on the lap of a very pale CJ, who was wiping sweat from his forehead. "Take deep breaths, Mr. CJ. You're safe now."

Mrs. Gage stood a little apart, observing the group. She had begun to open her heart the moment she had invited Danny Mac and Kenann into her life. They brought with them more people to love and lots of crazy adventures. She looked over at Pinky and Nita who represented her other life. Her heart was full of thankfulness and hope for the future.

Jake looked up at that moment and smiled at her. *Yes, my life is full.*

Once everyone had caught their breath, Carter called the president. He spent considerable time emphasizing the connection between this group, ISIS, and the gravity that entailed. He also impressed upon him the sensitive nature of having so many clandestine pipelines under the soil of friend and foe alike. This was going to take great diplomatic skill to keep it from falling into the wrong hands and becoming a worldwide power pandemic.

Nita and Pinky said their good-byes as they planned to accompany Paulo home to his family. Nita hugged Mrs. Gage, whispering something to her. Mrs. Gage emitted a throaty laugh. She put her arm through Pinky's and sent her regards to her royal-but-clueless husband.

The rest of the group waited until the choppers arrived to transport the captives to an undisclosed location. Several of the council had attempted to bribe Carter for their release and continued their ploy as they were led away by the Seal Team. Carter maintained all the information from the hard drives. He had transmitted it over secure channels to his team in Virginia and planned to carry the flash drives personally all the way home. The president asked Carter to stay with the captives for the next several days to oversee their debriefing. He had no time to say goodbyes and chided himself for even feeling he wanted to. He was a soldier for pity's sake. He nodded to the group as he followed the team to the waiting choppers and continued to chide himself for the lump he felt in his throat.

The small group returned to the chalet to pack. They then gathered in the formal living room of the chalet with whatever luggage they had as they waited for their transport to the airport. After all the excitement of the last several hours, they were very subdued, talking quietly in small groups.

Mrs. Gage's phone rang. She listened intently and spoke in low tones. She ended the call and addressed the group. "May I have your attention please? We have a few days before Blade must return home to school, and I have a small situation that needs to be addressed. Anyone game?"

She laughed out loud as the cacophonous roar of glee erupted, and the merry band of misfits rushed to surround her.

EPILOGUE

CARTER WAS LAUDED in the halls of the White House for successfully taking down the leadership of this powerful secret society. He was told he could write his own ticket. He kept insisting that he did not do this alone but was told that the success of any team still reflected its leadership. Only he knew better. This, more than anything in his life, had humbled him. He had little to say about the operation and felt embarrassment when he got pats on the back.

Alone in his townhouse apartment in Georgetown, his mind drifted to the real heroes behind what happened. He also admitted to himself that he missed them. He wondered what all of them were doing and if they ever thought of him. Of course, thumb screws could not coerce him to ever admit it. He found himself daydreaming.

After several minutes pondering, he sat up from slouching on the couch. *It might just work*, he mused. He felt better already.

Blade was back in school and had finally finished all his work from the weeks he had been away. He convinced CJ (which did not take much) to get a small place in town. When he was not on the road, he could come home to him. Blade would never know what that meant to CJ when he said it. He found a small house on the same street as Blade and his mother, Leticia, who also seemed to be very pleased with the new arrangement.

Mrs. Gage anticipated Granny's desire to move to Memphis and asked her to come live with her.

At first, Granny opposed the idea. "I can't live *here*!"

"And why not?" Mrs. Gage challenged.

"Well, it's…it's—oh, I don't know! Why would you want me to?"

"You're a good company. I don't have to pretend anything with you. You are not pretentious and you enjoy a good chat, a belly laugh, and an occasional glass of wine. Why wouldn't I want you here?"

"Are you sure, Gabrielle? I don't want to be a bother."

"Now stop talking nonsense. Call your neighbor and tell him you will be staying here for the time being. See if he will continue to watch your place for you, all right?"

"All right. This is very kind of you. I appreciate this."

"You should know by now I never do anything I don't really want to do."

That was true, Granny thought and wondered what Mrs. Cage had up her sleeve.

Since their return, Judy and Andy had spent the time letting their families know of their marriage. Judy's parents were rather shocked at the news but hurried to hide it and welcomed Andy in true Arkansas fashion. Food and family were assembled in record time, and the party began. Andy and Judy were both relieved and thought, *One down, one more to go.*

On the flight to Arlington, Virginia, Judy could feel the tension steadily building in Andy. When she commented on it, he brushed it off as nothing. Just nerves heading back into the bustling Beltway region. Her first clue regarding trouble was Andy's hesitance to call his mother that they were in town.

"Let's get settled first. I haven't been back to my flat since I left to kidnap you."

"Kidnap me?"

"Oh, wait! Didn't I mention that was plan *B*?"

"And I played right into your hands."

"Better than I could have dreamed." He emphasized that with a tender kiss in the back of the taxi.

She was pleased to not be horrified by a bachelor pad. Instead, it was a tasteful apartment in neutral tones and hardwood floors. She loved it. Because she knew he would, she had waited at the door for him to carry her across the threshold.

He hit the button on his stereo, took her jacket off, and pulled her into his arms. "Dance with me, Judy."

The next morning, Judy confronted Andy. "Call your mother."

He sighed. "Okay, but just remember, I tried to warn you."

He did not say much in the exchange except, "Yes, Mother."

They made arrangement to come for dinner at seven. Judy asked what she should wear and paled when Andy brought out a tuxedo.

He saw her look and got it. "Get your coat." He took her to a shop near his apartment and picked out a simple black dress that fit her like a glove. He completed the ensemble with shoes and a wrap. Because he never paid attention to things like that, he had to ask, "Do you have jewelry?"

"Okay, Andy, you have successfully lifted my nerves into panic mode."

He did not respond and picked out a strand of pearls and matching earrings. "Those will do."

They dressed in silence and did not speak on the drive to his family home. Judy's sharp intake of breath when she saw the lights of the grand home as they rounded a curve in the driveway had him looking at her.

Eyes narrowed, she said, "You could have said something."

"It's not who I am. It's who she is."

"Will she like me?"

"No." Before she could protest, he added, "She doesn't like anyone." He took her hand as they got out of the car and a valet drove the car away. Andy took in a deep breath and let it out slowly.

Judy put her arm through his. "Don't leave me alone in there."

"Not a chance, doll. You are my world now."

When Danny Mac found out Angelo had left his life in Brussels, he made arrangements for him to use one of the church's apartments they used for families in need. He had already secured employment with a computer company and was saving for a deposit on his own place. He had settled into the community and was feeling pretty good about life.

The church had their monthly fellowship dinner and decided to also welcome their elder, their preacher, and his bride home from their adventure. Granny let Kenann know she would be staying with Mrs. Gage for the time being.

"Granny, why didn't you say something? You could have the other apartment in our house."

"No, you kids need your space."

"Oh, Granny!"

"Why don't you all just keep both sides and turn it back into a single dwelling?"

Kenann appeared to consider this for the first time. "Actually, that's not a bad idea. I may need to do some remodeling. Want to help?"

"If I can fight international terrorists, I think I can knock out a wall or two."

Kenann laughed and pulled her into a hug.

"How're my girls doing?" Danny Mac brought them tall glasses of sweet ice tea.

"Granny had a great idea about us turning our apartments back into a full house. What do you think?"

"What will we do with all that space?"

"We can have people in for parties, and if we have kids, we will need the extra room."

Granny noticed Danny Mac's skin going pale and grinned to herself. *This man who can face down deadly enemies is scared of a baby.*

He cleared his throat. "Sure, sounds great! Why not?"

Kenann looked at her big tough guy and laughed. "My minister mercenary!" Then she kissed him on the cheek. They grinned at each other. She looked around and realized. "Where's Mrs. G?"

Granny answered, "She sent me on and said she would be along later. She had some *business.*" They all laughed.

As if on cue, the International Woman of Mystery breezed in the door. Jake held out his hand to her and she went straight to him, smiling. Kenann couldn't help but notice several of the widows from the church frowning into their pecan pies. Blade ran through the door of the fellowship room trailed by a smiling CJ Baer and Leticia. After several minutes of mingling, the group found their way together around a corner table.

Leticia asked for everyone's attention. "I know all of you love Blade like your own. But I am his mother, and I deserve to know what is going on." Her tone was not unkind, but it was very firm.

Everyone froze. Mrs. Gage reached across the table and put her hand over Mrs. Daniels. "You're absolutely right, Leticia. I have no real excuse. He has become such a part of our group, I guess we forget he is still a little boy."

Blade protested, "Mom!" She gave him *the look*.

Jake took over. "Leticia, it is a rather long story, but we have been involved in chasing down some bad guys over the last few months. Blade has been a big help."

"My little man?" She turned to Danny Mac. "Danny?"

"Yes, and I take full responsibility."

She sighed and looked at Blade. "Now what do you have to say?"

He squared his shoulders. "I wanted to help Danny Mac. He was in trouble. Then I found out I liked it, and I'm good at it, Mom." Leticia looked at the others. They nodded.

Danny Mac affirmed, "He is."

"Well, all I can say is you better keep him safe."

There was a collective sigh of relief. They all knew this could have gone very badly. And they also knew they would have deserved it. She then wanted to hear all about their adventures. She laughed, she cried, and she thumped Blade on the head. They were caught up in the storytelling when they became aware that the room had grown quiet. The group looked up; their eyes were drawn to the front of the room.

Carter stood in the doorway, flanked by Judy and Andy. No one moved. Carter moved to their table. Andy and Judy remained in the doorway. With the light from the hall at their back, they looked like avenging angels. "Come along, misfits. It's time for a council of war."

CPSIA information can be obtained at www.ICGtesting.com
Printed in the USA
BVOW06s0635120716

454887BV00007B/4/P

9 781683 015147